Bitter Return

Luke Coyle had seen a mountain of violence in his young life. He had cared for the wounded and the dying and buried more men than he could remember. Yet he still held a secret doubt as to his own courage.

Only when he threw in his lot with a man who seemed to have lost everything did his own life begin to make sense. They rode together into a dark past in search of understanding and found there enemies who sought to destroy all memory of an evil deed and every voice of protest with deadly gunfire.

As flame and smoke filled the winter air and blood soaked into the snow, the innocent would die alongside the guilty.

Bitter Return

BILL MORRISON

A Black Horse Western

ROBERT HALE · LONDON

© Bill Morrison 2006
First published in Great Britain 2006

ISBN-10: 0-7090-7909-5
ISBN-13: 978-0-7090-7909-5

Robert Hale Limited
Clerkenwell House
Clerkenwell Green
London EC1R 0HT

Typeset by Derek Doyle & Associates, Shaw Heath.
Printed and bound in Great Britain by
Antony Rowe Limited, Wiltshire

1

'Goddamn!'

Jed Parker halted as he struggled towards the daylight entering the narrow mine-shaft. He lowered the wooden crate to the trampled dirt at his feet and turned to glance back at his companion who had halted with stooped shoulders in the deeper shadows behind, pickaxe in one hand and a shovel in the other.

'You would hardly believe this, Web, but I've gone and left my watch in there! Be a buddy, will ya, and go back in for it. It's on thet little shelf jest past the third turning.'

'It's as dark as hell back there.'Web grinned. 'What do you think I am – a goddamned owl, or what?'

Web, in spite of his complaint was good-humoured, as always. He leaned the shovel against the rock wall and put one hand to his greying hair in an attempt to scratch some of the dirt from it. His face had become lined with the passage of his forty-five years but there were creases near his mouth left by the ready smile which had been an abiding feature since his far-off youth, in spite of a life which had brought more hardships than comforts.

Parker looked at him and smiled in return but without reflecting the glimmer of light which danced in his partner's eyes. Both were grey-eyed, a fact Parker had noted with more than an ordinary degree of interest. Also, they were about the same height and build but Parker was balding a little.

Parker stared hard at his mining-partner, trying to look past the dark, crumpled clothes under the layer of grey dust and into Web's mind. As always he came to the rapid conclusion that there was little there. Web was easy-going, trusting and good-humoured in a way that he, Jed Parker, could never be. It was the merest accident that had brought them together – just a casual conversation in a saloon and Web's frank admission that he had with him a month's pay from cattle-driving. Parker had been quick to seize the chance of gaining enough money and some physical help in this last hope of striking it rich in gold-mining. In that way they had come to be partners. Now, though, the hope of finding gold had faded as far as Parker was concerned but – as he was fond of saying to himself – there were other fish to fry.

His narrow mouth twitched slightly under his dark moustache as if he appreciated Web's joke.

'What the hell, Web, you could find a black cent in a cartful of coal-dust! Thing is, the watch is sure enough on thet little shelf of rock just about elbow-high. You can't miss it! I'll take all this gear back outside and I'll even boil you up some coffee, if you take any time over it. Seriously, though, it won't take ya more than a couple of minutes and you can see better than me – what with my eyesight and the lamp gone out and all! What do ya say, partner?'

'All right! All right,' answered Web, in mock irritation, 'but get on the coffee! I'm about as thirsty as an alligator in the desert!'

He turned and began to make his way back along the way he had just come. He bent his head as he went as the roof was low and he was a tall man in spite of a permanent stoop. The darkness seemed to fall upon him as soon as he turned his back on the light from the mine entrance and within a few steps he was forced to feel his way with his tough hands on the hard roughness of the hacked wall.

His progress slowed with every yard but he knew when he had come to the first and then the second bend. It was hard going in the pitch-dark and he cursed a couple of times under his breath but his usual good nature did not desert him. He had come along this tunnel often over the weeks in the daily work of mining. Jed had been so sure from the start that the old seam, long since deserted by an earlier generation of miners, must lead on to more gold but so far it had not turned out like that and they had gained nothing from all their labour. Jed had tried dynamite too, but apart from bringing down a great deal of rock there had been nothing to show for it.

Still, he seemed to know a lot about mining and continued to speak as if they might strike lucky yet. In his heart, Web no longer believed it would happen but he had not said so. The thought did not depress him in anything like the way he believed it must affect his partner, who – in spite of his superior airs at times – had evidently had little luck in anything he had tried throughout life.

In that way, sure, his experience had been much the same as that of Web who had spent much of his life wondering where his next meal was likely to come from.

Life was changing however, for Web, who could now look forward to a marvellous future in which his partner could not share. There was light at the end of even this dark tunnel and Web could not help but grin in the dark at the thought of it.

He felt his way round the third corner of the shaft and put his hand out to touch the narrow stone shelf he knew was there. His fingers searched carefully along its surface but felt nothing but the harsh rock. That was strange. Jed was a careful man who rarely made mistakes However, he had got things wrong this time – or maybe he had not. The watch might have fallen to the rock floor under the narrow ledge. If so, it might have been damaged which would be a disaster for Jed, who seemed to prize it above most things.

Web lowered himself carefully to the ground and passed his hands all round; there was nothing there but pieces of stone. Gingerly, he rose up again, making sure he did not thump his head, and moved further along the shaft, feeling his way by inches.

The tunnel was narrowing as he entered the most recently excavated section and he began to feel as if he was heading into a dark pit leading to the bowels of the earth. It was like creeping into hell, he thought, grinning at the idea, but with his mind a little troubled.

It occurred to him that if Jed's watch was indeed on the ground, then there was a pretty good chance he could stand on it with his heavy boots; that would be a dark day for Jed and for himself too, as there was no doubt he would feel bad about it, whether he was really to blame or not. Anyway, it could not be helped as he was as blind as a bat and could not feel anything much with his feet.

He turned slowly, realizing the futility of the search, and crept a few steps back the way he had come. In his heart, he was eager to see again the light of day but he did not hasten for he had learned how easy it was to injure oneself in this mine with its sharp edges of rock ready to rip hands and elbows and boulders waiting to be tripped over.

What a pity it was that he did not have the lamp with him. That would have solved everything. But Jed had snuffed it out as soon as daylight had appeared in the short distance ahead. That was unusual for Jed who was not too concerned about saving a small quantity of oil.

It was queer too, he thought, that Jed's watch was not where he said it was. That watch was Jed's most valued possession. Always, he wore it in his waistcoat, where it shone against the dark blue cloth. Jed was a smart dresser when he was not working and wore a leather jacket with fancy fringes on the sleeves and a dark hat which was always clean and brushed, just like himself.

He never dressed like that, of course, when he worked in the mine. Always, he left his best clothes, boots, hat and even his watch in his tent outside . . . Now, that *was* weird! Why would Jed have brought his gold watch into the mine at all?

He stopped in the dark, greatly puzzled at the thought. Then he shrugged. So Jed, for once, had got things all wrong. He had, likely enough, never brought the watch in here! Almost certainly, it lay in the tent along with his clothes. Maybe he had found it already.

Well, he, Web, would have something to say about it. Before he got out of the mine he would have thought of some sharp remark to make that would bring a rueful grin to Jed's face and an apologetic shake to his head.

Suddenly he saw the funny side of it all, as irritation did not rise within him as it would have done with most men in such a situation.

He smiled in the darkness in his usual good-natured way but it was for the last time in his life. . . .

When Web walked into the darkness of the mine, Jed Parker watched him go and stood for a moment longer just in case he should change his mind for some reason. However, Web did not reappear and Parker turned and walked towards the bright light of the entrance. He left the wooden box he had been carrying and Web's shovel and pickaxe on the ground.

He walked without haste, almost as if he were counting each step, and made his way over to a spot where a large boulder stood out from the surrounding stands of rock. He turned then and looked back at the mine entrance. It looked like a dark cave against the rocky landscape that surrounded it. There was nothing much in the immediate area but boulders and scrub and the rugged shape of the stony hillside rising to the sky.

No one ever came here. There was nothing to come for unless you happened to be an optimistic gold-miner with more hope than common sense. As it happened, that was an advantage in the present situation. Nevertheless, he permitted himself a careful look round. He was a cautious man and was not inclined to take risks that he did not need to. All was quiet, however, as he had expected. There was no movement except for a couple of buzzards circling high overhead.

He lowered his gaze and drew his gold watch from the pocket of his jacket where he had hidden it that morning just after their usual breakfast of coffee and pork and biscuit. Web, he remembered, had been laughing and telling some yarn about cow-punching. Parker had smiled too but with his mind on other things.

He counted off the last few seconds as he observed the little black hand move round inside the circle of gold sparkling in the sunlight. Then he moved a wooden board that he had previously placed against the boulder to hide the dynamite charger. In his mind he saw Web feeling over that little rocky ledge in the pitch dark. With no further hesitation, but with practised skill, he pressed down the handle.

The explosion reverberated through the hillside but caused no disturbance except for a small avalanche of stones down the slope and a mighty cloud of dust from the mouth of the mine. Parker had planned it that way. He intended bringing down the roof and had placed a charge well calculated to do just that.

He stood still for several minutes as he watched the dust settle. No emotion showed on his features. He felt nothing but a sense of quiet satisfaction.

He replaced his watch in his pocket and walked slowly to the mouth of the mine. Fresh dust was everywhere but when he peered inside he could see that the tunnel was blocked. He looked around and found the long length of fuse he had hidden the day before when Web had still been in town, buying supplies for them both. The township lay about twenty miles distant and Web had ridden off on his errand cheerfully enough, pleased at the change in routine. Parker had made good use of the time by placing his charge and concealing the long fuse so that even a suspicious man would not have been likely to notice it – and Web was not that kind of man.

He gathered up what remained of the evidence and then walked over to the two tents pitched a short distance away. The one with the patches on top was Web's. Inside lay Web's clothes – not much to look at but a little better than those he wore in the mine. His jacket held his wallet containing various letters and a document from a lawyer's office. Parker had seen them before. Web had been as trusting as a day-old puppy and his new-found happiness had caused him to open up his heart even further than usual.

What had puzzled Parker at first was why Web had decided to stay on as his partner in this pretty hopeless mining venture. Then, to his amazement, he realized that the good news had come when Web and he were at Smoky Hill buying supplies and getting ready to hit the trail. Web had gone to the mail office and collected his letter. He had come back with an expression of disbelief on his face although he had said nothing further at the time.

Later, after they had started mining, Web had burst out with the news and it was then that Parker realized that Web was still there only because he had promised to join in the venture and did not want to let his partner down. Web did not need anything from the mine now but had decided to stay on for a while because he could not go back on his word.

It was an astonishing decision. Parker could

not understand it. It was foreign to his own way of thinking. Guys like Web were too good for this world. They ought to be in heaven or someplace amongst their own kind!

Well, that had all been arranged now. Parker grinned at his own dry humour as he read through the letters in Web's wallet and then placed them carefully in his own pocket. He rummaged through the rest of Web's belongings, which were few, and decided to get rid of them as they were not worth keeping. Only the rifle was of any value, an old Henry repeater with Web's name, Harry Webster, carved into the stock. It was a useful weapon and having the name carved on it was a bonus.

The rest of the stuff, including the tent, could be thrown into the narrow ravine nearby where it would be unlikely ever to be found. He set about carrying out the task and listened to the thump and rattle as Web's gear vanished and hit the rocks below. He then went back to his own tent and shaved off his moustache. The act was probably unnecessary but he felt it to be an extra safeguard and helped to settle his mind.

Having got rid of Web's gear, he looked at the horses. There were two, a roan and a skewbald. The roan, Billy, had belonged to Web and

16

he decided to keep it as it seemed in better condition than his own. The reason was simply that it had been better looked after but that did not occur to Parker. The other horse and the two mules he would sell at the first opportunity.

He stood for some minutes looking round at the campsite he had shared with Web for some weeks. For a brief moment he thought of Web inside the mine workings under the rubble and wondered how much was left of him. He guessed – not much. The idea did not trouble him. They had worked and eaten and talked together but it meant nothing to Parker. He had never been able to relate to other people. He was unaware of the fact, imagining that other folks were the same. He was glad to be rid of Web, not that Parker had anything against his partner, but Web needed to be out of the way so that Parker could move on.

He noted that marks had been left in the earth indicating where the tents had been pitched. He kicked them out and did what was possible to remove the other signs of activity in the vicinity of the mine. It might be better if some casual passer-by did *not* notice that the mine had been reopened. A fall of rock was a natural enough thing in itself and anyone looking into the shaft would just move on without suspicion. He had chosen the best method. A bullet in the back from his sidegun would have required investigation if Web had ever been found. As it was, Web had been buried at the moment of his death, which was smart thinking on the part of Parker.

It was time to go. He saddled up Web's roan and packed the small amount of gear on to the mules. Then he rode slowly away from the mine, allowing the horse to find its own footing over the rough ground. He had to get to this place called Oakfield. It was mentioned in all of Web's letters and in the legal document. In his casual-sounding conversations with Web he had discovered that it lay about a hundred miles to the north near a river called Teal. Web had not been there for many years but he had a pretty good idea where it was. Parker was certain that he would have little difficulty in finding it himself.

As he rode away from the camp the rain began to fall. It was the first time for months but it was just about that time of year when downpours could be expected. He pulled his jacket collar up over his neck and tugged his black hat over his brow. He did not mind the rain. It was refreshing after the long dry spell and he knew it would wash away any traces left of the recent camp.

He turned things over in his mind as he went. He felt sure that all would go well. Life was going to take a turn for the better: he would be able to stand up taller and spit when he felt like it.

The idea pleased him and he laughed genuinely for the first time in years.

2

The wind and rain swept through Smoky Hill as it had been doing for three days, spattering like lead shot on the roofs and sidewalks and the timbers of the buildings, causing folks to close up their shutters and to remain indoors as much as was possible. The main street that had remained all summer under a carpet of dust was turned now to mud. A pool lay by the general store. A little river of water ran down the slope that led from the gate of the timber and stone church.

A few horses stood patiently enough at the hitching-posts, waiting until their owners had finished some essential errand or other, before being led once again into shelter, as would be the case since horses were valuable pieces of property and not to be put at risk from chilling when there was no need.

There were quite a number of horses in Smoky Hill. It was not what some people would have described contemptuously as a 'one-horse town'. There was also a livery stable and a sheriff's office and a jail besides the church and graveyard. The livery stable was generally busy enough. The stage changed horses there when it came through once a week and there were always mounts to be hired by any citizen who needed one.

Luke Coyle worked in the livery stable. He had been there for three of his twenty-five years ever since he decided to leave Squaw Creek The work was tedious and dirty, with no future and no present and, what made it worse, in his case, no past worth looking back upon.

He was tall, with sandy hair, worn too long, which hung almost to his shoulders. Once in a while he went to the barber to have it cut a good deal shorter. At other times, when he felt he could afford to do nothing else, he cut it himself with his razor. Lately he had been feeling too depressed and downhearted to do anything with it.

Any skilled doctor who might have been consulted would have been of the opinion that Luke was suffering a bit from depression. Not that he would ever have consulted a doctor about that. He knew well enough how he felt and the reasons for it.

There were few days when he did not think about Squaw Creek and about the war. Some years ago, the worst of his memories were of the bitter conflict he had witnessed, but just as bitter now were the memories of his home town.

He tried not to think of the war but it was rarely out of his mind or out of his dreams. He had killed no one throughout the long four years he had spent in uniform, a fact for which he was thankful but which had added to the weight that threatened, often enough, to burden down his mind.

When, at long last, the war had reached its end, he had returned with rising hope to Squaw Creek On the outskirts of that little town was the tiny farm on which he had spent his childhood. The first shock had been to find that his widowed mother had died in his absence, but he had set to with determination to put the place to rights as, he felt sure, many another ex-soldier was doing throughout the country.

That endeavour, however, was not enough. Squaw Creek had changed and not for the better. There were other young men who had survived the war and had been hardened and made restless by it. They had learned to shoot to kill and to use the bayonet and some of them saw themselves as heroes and hard men who needed to pay little attention to the attitudes and needs of others. The result was much drunkenness and wild shooting in and around the town, where any helpless dog that they reckoned might just happen to be rabid or any window owned by a person who objected to their rowdiness was likely to become a target for their sideguns, which they now wore low on the hip as if they had ambitions to be like the gunslingers who abounded in some parts of the West.

In a way, Luke could understand it. The war had affected everyone mixed up in it in one way or another. These particular fellers were, however, taking it all the wrong way. He had known most of them since boyhood and hoped that after a time they might come to see sense. He even remonstrated with them and that had been a mistake because they resented his criticism and began looking for ways of getting even with him.

He had not made any secret of the part he had played in the war. He had done no actual fighting, being employed almost the whole time as a stretcher-bearer. He had walked through fields of dead and dying and had seen corpses by the hundreds placed in rough coffins or buried sometimes in sheets or rags in mass graves. He had done the work well enough, always with reverence and without complaint and was reckoned by his superiors to be good at it. For that reason he had remained in such employment and had seen relatively little of the actual cut and thrust of battle. Rather, he had seen it in all the mutilated corpses he handled, and heard it also in the screams and groans of the dying.

To his surprise these rowdies in Squaw Creek, irritated by his attitude towards them, seized upon his experience as an excuse for baiting him whenever he appeared in town. The contemptuous yells of 'stretcher-bearer!' and 'burial party!' followed him down the street. It was just foolishness as there was no doubt that if any of them had needed a stretcher on the field of battle, they would have been only too glad to see him. He had tried to shrug it off but that wasn't so easy. He felt too raw and sensitive after his war experience to accept their hostility with equanimity.

Secretly he was also troubled by his own behaviour on the one occasion when he had found himself face to face with the enemy. The Confederates had launched an attack one day on the camp where he was working as a medical orderly. Like his comrades, Luke had snatched up a musket but when he found himself with a clear shot at a Reb about to climb a fence, Luke had missed by a yard. He knew within himself that the miss was deliberate. He also knew that if his comrades had behaved in the same way then the camp would have been taken. As it was the Confederates were driven off.

It was clear dereliction of duty on his part, although nobody was aware of it. Time and again he had asked himself why and always he came up with the same answer. It was simply that the idea of adding another corpse to the countless numbers he had already seen was too much to bear.

That secret memory and the ceaseless verbal abuse from the swollen-headed young veterans eventually became too much for him. The yells and insults and reminders of the war just wore him out. He became angry too, and there were times when he even felt tempted to use the old Colt revolver that had belonged to his father. Eventually, he had had enough and decided to sell off what little stock he had and leave the town. It seemed to him that there was nothing to stay for.

As he fed oats to his charges over those wet days of late summer such thoughts were more than ever in his mind. There were folks in Smoky Hill who would have reckoned him a coward if they had known of his past but he had told them nothing. He was not sure whether he could be regarded as a coward or not. It was a thought he wrestled with on a daily basis.

'Hey, Luke!' Sam Dewar, boss of the livery stables, shouted at him from the doorway, arousing him out of his reverie. 'You seen thet pesky Injun, Catfish? He ain't appeared all day!'

'No, never have,' answered Luke, like a dreamer awakening.

'What about you, Bitty?'

Fred Bitford, the third employee in the stables, shrugged his narrow shoulders without looking up. 'Nope, not me neither.'

Bitty, middle-aged and greying, had lost his wife and daughter to the fever years earlier and had never forgiven God or the world. He spoke only to answer direct questions.

'If Catfish don't come in today, he kin look elsewhere for work!' snapped Dewar, returning to his quarters attached to the stables. 'Them goddamned Injuns! Never know where they git to!'

Catfish, old-looking, with a face lined by a lifetime of hardship, had earned his name because he seemed to have the knack of catching that kind of fish in the creeks some miles out of town. His real Indian name was unpronounceable to the citizens of Smoky Hill. He was generally held in a degree of contempt by the respectable townsfolk but Luke liked him well enough and regarded him as a friend.

Luke felt a little concerned. It would be a bad business for Catfish if Dewar kept his promise. An elderly Indian would not find it easy to find other work. Luke had not seen him since Saturday when they had finished at the stables. Yesterday, being the Sabbath, was not a day when Catfish would come into town. He did not attend church and was not expected to. Luke, for that matter, did not attend either, as the minister still gave thanks for victory in the war and Luke could not see much victory in it for anyone. Fred Bitford made a point of not going because he could not forgive God for the tragedy that had afflicted him.

Nevertheless, Catfish ought to have been at work today. Maybe he was ill. Or worse, he might be drunk, for which there was no excuse in the eyes of his employer.

The rain eased as the afternoon wore on and Luke decided to find out what was wrong with Catfish and tell him of Dewar's displeasure. He rode his piebald pony out of town and after about a couple of miles, arrived at the 'Catfish residence' as it was sarcastically called by the town wits. It was no more than a poor shack built from old wood by Catfish a good many years before. The roof leaked and there was only one window, which was boarded up by Catfish's wife in the evenings.

She was called Mary Elk and was more worn out in appearance even than her husband. Unlike him, she was actually happier in her present situation than she had ever been with an Indian band following buffalo over the prairies. The work of a squaw, she remembered, had been tough. The heavy tepee had been dismantled and then re-erected by the women with every change of camp. These changes had been frequent. In addition, there had been buffalo to skin and butcher, clothes to make from hides, buffalo-chips to collect for fuel, fires to carry from place to place, endless cooking, even moccasins to chew in order to make them soft. Also, there had been the ever-present possibility of attack from strange and hostile Indians, likely to end in sudden and painful death.

This shack at least had the virtue of never needing to be moved. Food, little enough though it was, came mostly from the general store in convenient parcels, never needing to be skinned. Only the catfish caught by her husband needed to be gutted and prepared but she did not mind doing that as it tasted good and was a welcome addition to their diet.

Luke found her standing at the door of the shack, looking out anxiously as she heard the sounds of his arrival.

'Mary!' called Luke.' We haven't seen Catfish all day. He ill or somethin?'

'No, Catfish not ill. He out somewheres. Rode out yesterday. Came back for rope.'

'Rope?'

'Yeah. Rope. An' he took the bread we had an' water an' fish we had for dinner.'

Luke dismounted, staring at her in surprise.

'What for? What's he doing? Where did he go?'

'Went out Boulder Ridge. He say man in hole. Hollering. You think Catfish mad now, Mister Luke?'

'When did he come back? I mean for this rope and the food?'

'He away all yesterday. Came back at sun-up. Then he just go. Could be crazy man now. That goddamned stables make him mad!'

'Could be,' grinned Luke feelingly, then looked serious again. 'What did he say about the man in the hole?'

'Nothin', Jest hollering. Catfish hardly spoke, Jest went off. Like in mad hurry.'

'Boulder Ridge?

Luke knew of it. He had ridden there several times over the past three years. It was as barren as its name suggested. There could be no fishing there but Catfish might have passed it on his way to the creek some miles beyond. He looked carefully at Mary, realizing that she had told him all she knew, and made up his mind to ride out that way himself. Probably he could get there before sundown.

As things turned out the sun was beginning its swift descent as he began the slow climb up the slope of the ridge. After a time he caught sight of Catfish in the distance, standing near the top of the ridge with his pony tethered nearby. The old Indian had his back turned to Luke and seemed to be staring at the ground. His head and shoulders and arms were drooping in an attitude that suggested exhaustion and defeat. He turned round only when Luke had approached very near to him, although there was little doubt that he had heard the pony from some distance away. Catfish missed very little but usually pretended a certain unawareness, a trick he had learned as a youth when trying to outwit his foes which had now become a habit.

'Hey, Catfish,' called Luke as he dismounted, 'I hear from Mary that you've got trouble. She said about some guy stuck in a hole. Is thet right?'

Catfish looked round and nodded, his eyes lighting up at the sight of Luke. He liked Luke, partly because the young feller had always shown him friendship but mostly because he was aware that Luke had more troubles in his mind than he ever made mention of.

'It's right,' he answered in his guttural tones. 'There is a man down there. In thet hole. I been trying to git him out all day. It ain't easy.'

Luke walked over with some degree of caution and saw the hole in the rock. It looked new, as if it had been split open recently. The stone looked fresh, unaffected by dirt or moss. The hole was about a yard across. There was still a little rivulet of rainwater running into it. It was too dark to see far down but it seemed deep. There was a rope hanging into it, one end of which Catfish had evidently tied around a large boulder.

'How in hell did he git down there?' asked Luke in amazement.

'Search me,' grunted Catfish. 'He don't know hisself.'

'He been there all this time – about a couple of days?'

31

'He reckons longer but . . .' Catfish tapped his own forehead, 'could be crazy.'

Luke lay on his chest and peered downwards into the hole. It was as dark as pitch. The sun was going fast and casting long shadows over the landscape.

'You all right down there?' yelled Luke, recognizing even as he did so the absurdity of the question.

'Git me out of here, will ya?' The answer came faintly from below, agitated, almost hysterical. 'I'm dying! Hey, you a white man? Thet Injun cain't seem to do nothin'.'

'He's doing his best,' answered Luke. He glanced at Catfish. 'He got thet rope tied around him?'

'Don't know. I tell him to but I guess not.'

Luke pulled at the rope and soon realized it hung loosely in the hole.

'Hey, tie the rope round your waist. Then maybe we kin help.'

'I got an injured hand! There's no feeling in it.'

'All right, I'll ride back into town to git help.'

'No, don't!' the voice rose into near hysteria. 'This is like hell! I've been in the dark for . . . seems like all my life . . .' The voice sank to a groan. 'All my life, God, what does that mean?'

The sun was declining rapidly, flooding the west in red. In a moment or two it would be nightfall. Luke remembered there would be no moon that night and riding back to Smoky Hill could be a difficult and hazardous task Anyhow, the man seemed panic-stricken at the idea of being left alone or even with Catfish.

'All right, we'll stay,' Luke shouted, 'but we can't git you out until morning. You ate thet food Catfish brought you?'

'Some of it. The rest dropped into the stones and I couldn't git to it.'

'Too bad. You badly hurt, do you reckon?'

'Cuts but they've stopped bleeding. My hand feels stove in.'

'What happened to ya? You climb right down there, or something?'

'I don't know! I've already told the Injun all that! I woke up in the dark, feeling like I'd been mixed up in a stampede. Rocks everywhere. I tried to climb out but could hardly move. All I could see was a little bit of sky 'way up there. Even saw a goddamned bird flying! Then the Injun came but then he went away and left me!'

Luke glanced at Catfish in the dying light, wondering why he had not ridden all the way into town for help instead of stopping short at his shack. But he already knew the answer.

Catfish knew very well how he was regarded by the townsfolk and would not ask them for help if he reckoned he might not need it The Indian had a lot of pride, which sometimes interfered with his common sense.

Luke realized that they had a long night ahead of them. Neither he nor Catfish would get much sleep. The man at the bottom of the hole would see to that. He had been in the dark long enough. If there was no light then at least he had to hear human voices.

'What's your name, friend?' Luke asked, yelling down into the dark. 'I'm Luke, this here's Catfish.'

There was a long hesitation then the answer came faintly, carrying at first a strong element of doubt which, nevertheless, quickly grew into conviction. 'Billy – the name's Billy.'

'All right, Billy. We'll get you out in the morning. It's the best we can do.'

Luke spoke to the trapped man for much of the night, asking time and again what had happened but always getting the same answer. Billy had regained consciousness in the pitch dark, feeling bruised and with an injured hand. He had lain for a long time in fear, until hope had come in the shape of Catfish. He had no idea of how he came to be in the hole. He did

34

not know anything about his past life. Too many questions seemed to upset him further, so Luke put in the time talking about Smoky Hill and a little about his own life until, with relief, he heard the man snoring.

In the morning light they hauled him out. Catfish attached the rope to both horses and Luke climbed down into the hole, hand over hand, until he reached the man below. There he tied a loop round Billy's waist and began the slow hard climb, using his feet on the rough walls and guiding the injured man's feet into places where there was a foothold.

Overhead, Catfish kept the horses under perfect control and led them forward a very few steps at a time, keeping the rope taut. Eventually, Billy lay on his back on the bare rock, staring at the sky with relief gradually replacing anxiety in his eyes.

Luke saw him clearly for the first time. He was a man of about forty years, tall, greying, and with lined features. His clothing was dark and dirt-covered.

'Tell you what, Billy,' said Luke kindly. 'Jest you lay there for while. Catfish will give you a drink. I'll see ya pretty soon.'

He walked back to the hole and looked at the surrounding rock, which seemed newly split and still dangerous. It could open up further any time. He frowned in puzzlement and then glanced over the edge of the high boulders nearby. About thirty feet below there was a flat space surrounded by scrub and a few stunted trees.

Without speaking again to his companions he clambered down the steep slope and walked over the open space. As he had guessed, there was an opening in the hillside. It was obviously the entrance to a mine. He was not surprised, having heard that there was an old gold-mine hereabouts. When he glanced into the opening, he saw that the shaft was completely blocked by fallen rock.

Well, it explained what had happened to Billy but there was nothing else there – no sign of mining operations, not even a horse standing around waiting for its owner. The whole area seemed to have been cleared. The rain had helped in that as Billy's footprints, if he had left any, would have been washed away by now.

Still, it was queer. There should be some sign of Billy having been around. Even if he had not been mining but had merely looked into the mine out of curiosity, there ought to have been a horse or at least some sign of one. But there was nothing but flat earth beginning to dry out after the rains.

Luke walked over the open space, eyes down. Then he stiffened and bent to pick up a short piece of rope. It was thin but strong, the kind of material used for a tent-guy. The strange thing about it was that it had not begun to rot even though it was lying out in the open. It was not new but had probably been in use fairly recently. But there was nothing else. The campsite had been cleared as if to destroy any sign of its existence.

Luke stared at the piece of cord and then slipped it into his pocket. He frowned thoughtfully as he climbed back up the slope. Who else had been here besides Billy?

When he reached the top he found Catfish easing Billy up into the saddle of the pony. Luke ran forward to help. The Indian turned to him, face twisted in exasperation.

'How come this feller cain't remember anythin'? Seems like he was jest born,' he whispered. 'He crazy?'

'Nope, jest a touch of amnesia. He's lost his memory. Could be jest temporary.' He had come across two cases of amnesia in the war, both soldiers who had been almost killed by cannon fire. He did not remember that either had recovered but maybe they did later. 'Hey, Billy, what's your second name? You're Billy what?'

There came a long silence. Billy's face worked convulsively, then brightened a little.

'Oakfield,' he said, with a hint of triumph. 'Name's Billy Oakfield.'

He seemed pleased. It was as if he was greatly relieved to find an identity for himself.

'Oakfield, eh,' murmured Luke. He had not met anyone of that name before but it seemed vaguely familiar. Maybe it really was Billy's name but maybe not. But there was something else that seemed more important right now – who was the other man who had been at the mine?

3

Jed Parker took the best part of two weeks to reach Oakfield, partly because he did not know the way but mainly because the weather was taking a turn for the worse, bringing sleet and light snowfalls, warning of an early winter. Travel was cold and slow but he got by well enough by seeking overnight lodgings in farmhouses and isolated cabins.

He was pleased at last to arrive at the town and rode up the main street to the small hotel where he sought a room and a bath and a meal. He could have found a room at one of the saloons in town at a cheaper rate but he did not want to give any impression that he was short of cash, although, in fact, that was the truth of his situation.

Nevertheless, he visited one of the saloons

that same evening, knowing that that was where he would be most likely to meet local people interested in conversing with a stranger. He bought a few drinks for the other customers in the bar and introduced himself as Harry Webster. That raised a few eyebrows but no suspicion. No one present remembered Harry, who had left the district many years before. The more personal matter relating to the reasons for his departure had been forgotten by everyone except one old feller who sat alone, drinking morosely. He, as it turned out, was called Eddie Hunt. He remembered having heard something about the quarrel between the two brothers at Goldcrest but said nothing, feeling it would be impolite and probably risky to mention it.

The worthwhile result of the evening, from Parker's point of view, was that he established himself as Harry Webster in the minds of a good many of the locals and also, by careful questioning, found out where Goldcrest actually lay. There were, after all, some things that Harry might be expected to remember even after such a long absence.

Next morning Parker visited the lawyer who had written the formal letter that was now carried, with a few more personal ones from Harry's brother, in the large pockets of a new sheepskin coat he had just purchased. He had bought the garment partly because of the inclement weather but also with a view to giving himself an air of prosperity and perhaps respectability.

Mr Withers, the only lawyer in Oakfield, greeted his client with affability and listened sympathetically to the carefully rehearsed little speech about the terrible sadness felt at brother Eric's death and how awful it was that he, Harry, had not been in time for the funeral.

Withers knew perfectly well that the brothers had not met for many years and also had some inkling of the reasons for it but, like old Eddie Hunt, said nothing of the matter. Discussing personal relationships was not what he was being paid for.

'Well, I see that you have my letter with you, Mr Webster, and you have allowed me to see the other letters you received recently from your brother. There is no doubt, of course, as to your identity but could I ask you to place your signature on this document? It confirms your acceptance of the title-deeds of the estate and ensures that all will be well. Just a formality, of course!'

Nevertheless, he studied the signature with interest while Parker looked on with a tiny smile at the corners of his mouth. Writing Harry

Webster's signature was something he had practised well and he had no doubts regarding his
skill.

'Fine,' said Withers at length 'Do you happen
to have your birth certificate with you, Mr
Webster?'

'Nope,' smiled Parker, 'I haven't seen that in
years. I don't know that I ever saw it!'

'Few people have,' smiled Withers, 'especially
around here. Some citizens don't have one at all,
I'm quite sure. I can send away for a fresh copy
of yours, if you would like me to?'

'Good idea,' answered Parker, thinking that a
certificate bearing Harry Webster's name might
prove useful at some future time. 'You do that,
Mr Withers. I would sure appreciate it. Thanks
for all you've done. Send your bill up to
Goldcrest. It will be settled without delay.'

That afternoon he rode out to the Goldcrest
ranch. He rode slowly, keeping in mind what he
had learned from his new-found friends in the
bar. The country was under a thin blanket of
snow with a wind that reminded him of the
Yukon where he had searched unsuccessfully for
gold many years before.

In the late afternoon he saw the place in the
distance. He was immediately struck by the size
and fine appearance of the building. It

reminded him vaguely of mansion houses he had seen in the South before the war, built with some degree of extravagance and with a view to making an impression on folks rather than to be strictly functional.

The lands belonging to Eric Webster and, before him, to his father, Jesse, were, Parker had gathered, pretty extensive too. Web had been coming in for a good inheritance. There was no doubt about that. Now all that had changed. Parker smirked to himself at the thought. Poor old gullible Web was buried for ever but now the fresh, smart 'Web' was riding in to claim what was legally his.

There were few animals in the fields but winter was certainly coming in so he gave the matter little thought. He wondered though how many staff remained on the ranch to keep things going until the new boss arrived. Well, he would soon find out.

The trail running in the direction of the house was almost obliterated by snow but he kept to it by careful riding. He passed a few shacks along the way, most of them some distance off the trail. A couple of times he saw people watching him as he went by and he made a point of waving to them in a friendly manner.

He was within half a mile of the house when

he came to a cabin much closer to the trail. The wooden building looked in good shape and there was a paddock and a little stable in which the grey head of a horse could be seen looking out at the snow. There were a few fruit-trees also, now bare of leaves. It looked to Parker like a well-kept little farm, maybe belonging to the ranch. Two men were clearing snow from the pathway to the front door. They stopped and straightened up to look at him as he approached.

'Howdy!' called Parker in his friendliest tone. 'Jest the start of this snowfall, I guess. There'll be a lot more to come yet. Sure thing!'

Both men were about his own age, greying and lean, but fit, as their quick work with the shovels was proving. They were dressed in working-overalls and wore heavy coats against the cold. The taller of the two had a slight squint and his face twisted as he returned Parker's grin. They both nodded but did not speak. It was as if they guessed who he might be but waited for him to say so.

'My name's Harry Webster.' Parker smiled. He was getting used to the lie, almost as if he were beginning to believe it himself. The sooner he did believe it, the better, he realized. It would lessen the chance of making a slip of the tongue.

'I'm taking over here in place of my dead brother,' he added sadly. 'Sorry, I don't know you fellers at all. It's been a long time.'

For a moment neither man answered. They stared at him with some slight degree of apprehension, as if trying to size him up. It was then that he guessed, rightly, that they had been employees of Eric Webster and were wondering whether this new boss would keep them on at the ranch. The idea boosted Parker's confidence and he hastily dismounted to shake them by the hand.

'I'm sure glad to meet you guys,' he enthused. 'Eric told me he had some swell fellers working around the place!'

They introduced themselves as Gus and Crow. It was as if they did not have surnames. Crow spoke in a croaking manner, as his name seemed to suggest. Gus was the taller of the two, with the squint and the twisted smile.

'Glad to see you, Mr Webster,' he said. 'We've been keeping a look-out ever since Eric – the other Mr Webster – died and we heard thet his brother was a-comin'. Hope you like it here, real swell!'

'This your own place?' asked Parker, with interest. 'You keep it real neat.'

'Well, it's kind of our own place. Land belongs

to the ranch, of course,' explained Gus, 'but old Mr Jesse Webster always left it like as if it almost belonged to our family. This here's my brother, Crow.'

'Swell, I'm real glad to meet in with you fellers. You come up to the house later and we can discuss how things are going to work out. I'll see you all right, no doubt about that!'

He smiled, noting their relieved expressions, and went on his way, glad to have made a couple of allies but delighted most of all that they accepted him, without question, as the man he claimed to be.

A little further on he saw a cabin set some distance from the trail. Snow was beginning to pile up against its sides but it looked homely enough with smoke rising from its single chimney. In the doorway stood a young woman wearing a blue dress, too light for the weather although she had thrown a shawl over her shoulders. He guessed that she had just stepped to the doorway to look at him as he passed. Her hair was black and she looked pretty even at that distance. He smiled and waved a hand, determined to keep up his pretence of good nature and friendliness.

She did not respond but stared at him closely. The distance was a little too great to make out the expression in her eyes but he felt, somehow, that they were about as cold as the ice beginning to form on the fence-posts.

When Parker reached the house and let himself in with the large key the lawyer had given him, he was immediately impressed. It was a fine house with a hall and a dining-room and a kitchen and study on the ground floor and an oak staircase leading to the bedrooms upstairs. It was well furnished with expensive chairs and tables and a sofa from the East, and there were paintings on the walls, mostly of scenes of the Rocky Mountains and a few of buffalo on the plains.

After a quick look round he stood in the hall with an expression of wonder on his face and a sense of astonished delight rising in his heart. Slowly it was beginning to sink into his mind that it was all his. He was the master of this fine house and all the land round about.

He stood and allowed the feeling of triumph and sense of power to swell up inside him until it puffed up his whole being. His chest expanded visibly and his head lifted like that of a victorious champion about to receive his laurels.

His mind was still caught up in amazement and joy when he heard noises from the front of the porch and then a tap upon the door. When

he looked out it was to find Gus and Crow standing there with bunches of firewood in their
arms. Gus was grinning and nodding as if he
understood exactly what Parker had been thinking about.

'Jest thought we would bring in some wood
for the fire, Mr Webster. Crow, here, has jest put
your horse into the stable and seen to it. We'll git
a fire goin' in no time at all!'

He was as good as his word and very soon the
hall fire burned brightly and another was flick-
ering into life in the dining-room. A piece of
cloth containing cold ham, cheese and bread
was also unwrapped and placed on a plate
brought in from the kitchen.

'This is all a bit rough and ready, Mr Webster,
but it was all we could manage right now. Hope
you like it.'

Parker did like it. He was grateful for the heat
and the food but most of all for the attention he
was receiving from these two men, who were
obviously very anxious to please him.

'You guys are invaluable! I can see that! I hope
you'll stay with me and find me as fair as my poor
departed brother . . .' He allowed his voice to
trail off sadly at this point but then made a show
of rallying his better spirits. 'Anyway, I'll do
everything I can to make a success of things

around here and with your help, I'll do it.'

'Fine horse you've got there, Mr Webster,' croaked Crow. 'I've fed him and rubbed him down real good. What's his name?'

'Billy,' said Parker. 'That's it – Billy.' He halted in his speech, suddenly wishing he had thought of another name for the animal. It had seemed a good idea at the time to take Web's horse but it did carry a constant reminder of things he wished now to forget. 'Thanks, Crow. You two men are a great help.'

He looked at the cold ham and bread and cheese and then walked over to warm his hands at the fire. They stood looking at him as if awaiting further orders.

'That's all right, fellers,' he said pleasantly. 'There ain't no point in hanging around here right now. I bet you have better things to do. Tell you what, though, it seems to me that Eric must have had a bit of domestic help. Some woman come in, or something?'

'Well, Mrs Spence did for a while but she died,' answered Gus. 'Got fever a couple of years ago. Then Eric managed by himself until he became ill.'

'Nobody else around?'

'Well, there's Jenny Spence, the daughter, but she ain't interested. Refused to work in the house. She works sometimes in Oakfield in the hotel.'

'She thet gal in the cabin not far from here?'

'Thet's her.' Gus sounded embarrassed. 'Kind of moody, I reckon. Didn't take too kindly to Mr Webster, especially since her mother died.' He shrugged. 'Don't know why. Queer gal. Doesn't speak much at all.'

Parker nodded, remembering the sense of chill drifting towards him over the snow from that open doorway. The idea did not much trouble him. His own experience with women led him to expect little else. He had never been on good terms with any of them.

After Gus and Crow had made their departure, Parker went into the study and opened up the bureau, using the key he found in the top drawer. It contained a variety of papers, mostly bills for corn-seed and cattle and horse-feed. There was a letter too, in Eric's handwriting. It looked like the draft of a personal letter addressed to Harry. Parker read it with interest and recognized it as a letter he held in his own pocket although parts of it had been changed. On the whole, it seemed a little more formal and less affectionate than the copy that Harry Webster had finally received. Eric had obviously been at pains to re-establish a good relationship with his brother.

Parker's attention was immediately diverted from the letter to another document of much more interest. It was headed 'Goldcrest Mining Company' and was a report on the mines owned by the company and the excellent progress being made. It contained a detailed account of a new seam of ore that was very promising although a good deal of expenditure would be needed to develop it. It was dated some years earlier and was bright with optimism and promise.

Parker's spirits rose sky-high as he read through the document. Eric Webster was mentioned as a principal shareholder, which meant, of course, that his brother, Harry, was certain to take his place. Things seemed to Parker to be looking better and better. Good old Web had told him, in his usual open and trusting way, that the family fortune had been established upon gold-mining. The only thing he had not been open about was his own reasons for leaving all those years ago.

He searched further but found nothing more about Eric's business interests. Perhaps when he had become ill he had passed them on to his lawyer to look after. That could not have been Withers as he had made no mention of such matters to Parker. Probably lawyers hired to represent the mining company were entrusted with Eric's interests. Parker resolved to open negotiations with the company lawyers in the very near future.

Meanwhile, he was delighted to discover in a narrow space just under the top of the bureau a wad of ten-dollar bills. It came to a total of a hundred dollars. Just what he needed to tide him over until he could extract more wealth from the ranch.

He hummed to himself and was in a rare good humour as he went back to the fire to consume his meal of ham and cheese and bread. There would be much better fare very soon. He had no doubt of it.

At that very moment Jenny Spence was standing in her small front room, gazing out of the window over the glistening snow. Her pretty face was calm, as she was a girl who rarely showed her emotions, but her mind was in turmoil. Although, like every one else around the ranch, she had been watching out daily for Harry Webster to arrive, actually to see him had given her a greater shock than she had expected.

A few years earlier it would not have mattered as at that time her mother had told her nothing of the relationship between the Websters and herself. As her mother had lain in a fever, however, she had spoken wildly but more frankly than she had ever done before and some of the story had come out about the quarrel between the brothers all those years ago. At the time her mother had been young and beautiful and sought after by both young men. It had led to trouble. Guns had been drawn and Eric had taken a bullet in the shoulder. Had news of the fight reached the ears of the sheriff of Oakfield there was no doubt that Harry would have been arrested and eventually imprisoned. The citizens of the town wanted to establish a law-abiding community and gun-slinging was always stamped upon.

Old Jesse Webster had put a stop to the affair by sending his younger son, Harry, on his way – not for ever – Jesse was too fond of his sons for that – but just until tempers had cooled. He had not reckoned, however, on the savage resentment that had remained in the heart and mind of Eric.

Harry had not returned, but not, in fact – as Jenny now believed – simply because he wished to desert the woman he had wronged. The truth was he was convinced that Anne, the woman he had loved, had turned against him and had gone back East to live a new life as she had vowed to do and was now lost to him for ever. For years, that knowledge had weighed heavily but he had accepted her loss and his brother's enmity. He had always blamed himself but, in time, had lived life as well as he could with much of his old cheerfulness returning.

Had he known that his sweetheart had remained at Goldcrest he would undoubtedly have returned, in spite of his brother's anger. But he had no way of knowing that he had done more harm than he had imagined and Anne had stayed to have the child she was now expecting.

Jesse Webster had allowed her to stay, as was only right, and after his death, his son, Eric, although remaining aloof, had carried out his father's wishes.

Jenny knew part of the story now for the first time. Her mother, lying on her deathbed, had told her something else too. The name, Mrs Spence, was an invention. In the vicinity of Oakfield an unmarried lady could not have a daughter. The mythical Mr Jeremy Spence had spent a good many years away on business and then had been caught up in the war and killed. Some people believed it. Others, of a kindly turn of mind, pretended to.

Jenny had been staggered at her mother's words. The hurt and resentment weighed upon her mind. Now that Harry Webster had made his belated homecoming she found hatred in her heart. It was foolish, as she well knew. The past could not be helped but she felt it could not be left unnoticed.

She turned from the window to look into the mirror on the wall. Grey eyes stared back at her. They seemed full of hurt and anger.

4

Web was in darkness. It pressed upon him like a suffocating blanket, filling his eyes and choking his lungs. Thunder deafened him. Wild fear sprang to his mind like a screaming storm. His hands, outstretched, found only cold rock, against which he pressed in panic as a child, locked in a small cupboard, might press against the door.

His hands turned bloody as they found an edge of cold stone, running, as it seemed to him, to some roof which he thought high but which in a moment had struck him in the head and brought more blood to the darkness of his face.

His outstretched hands touched a loose stone and he pulled at it in desperation and felt it move. There were others too, seemingly piled in a black barricade before him, and he pushed and pulled until his hands turned raw. Then he saw light, a faint hint of day, and his heart rejoiced. He struggled more and more to bring it within reach. . . .

Then he saw overhead the grime-covered ceiling and the face of a woman.

She was Indian, old and ugly, with broad cheek-bones and a skin like old parchment, but there was kindness in her eyes and she smiled, showing broken teeth. Her rough hand was gripping his outstretched arm. She held on to him gently and then pushed his arm back to the blanket that lay in disarray across his body.

To his surprise he realized he was lying on a bed in the shack. He recognized the room as one he had seen before. He remembered the old stove in the corner and the ancient, tattered bearskin on the wall.

'You dream bad,' said the woman. 'Better wake.'

There came other sounds and two men appeared beside her. He knew he had seen both before. He even remembered their names. There was an Indian called Catfish and a young white man by the name of Luke. He remembered that they had pulled him out of the hole. He could not be sure when it had happened. It might have been a moment ago or many years in the past.

The young man called Luke stared at him thoughtfully and then smiled, a faint trace of relief coming into his features.

'You seem better now, Billy,' he remarked softly. 'Leastways, you look as if ya know where you are.'

Web looked startled. He pushed himself up on his elbows, while Luke put out a restraining hand.

'Oakfield? I've gotta go to Oakfield!'

'Yeah? Why is thet?' asked Luke. He felt immensely relieved. Oakfield was a place he had never heard of but it seemed to make more sense than a person's name. More important, it was evidence that Billy was getting back his memory. He stepped forward to look more closely into the bruised and cut face against the dirty pillow. 'You come from Oakfield?'

'Yeah.' Web fell back exhausted. 'How long have I been here?'

'Four days. You've been out cold most of the time but sometimes thrashing about in thet bed like a fish out of water.'

'Catfish mebbe,' grinned the grey-haired Indian beside him.

'What's so important about Oakfield?' persisted Luke. 'You got folks there?'

'Sure, sure.' Web's face seemed to brighten

for the first time and then collapsed in grief. 'But my father died.' He screwed up his eyes, struggling to think. 'When was it? No, no, thet was a long time past! I remember now! My brother, Eric! I got to see him! I promised! I gotta git back to Goldcrest!'

'Goldcrest?' asked Luke, 'What's that?'

'I was born there. It's a ranch – a swell ranch. Always belonged in my family.'

Luke's face showed his surprise. Then he nodded thoughtfully. Something was beginning to make sense. Billy came from a rich family. Maybe that had something to do with this. Money could always bring complications.

'What happened at the mine, Billy?' he asked quietly.

'Roof fell in.' Web looked distressed. 'Must have been an accident.'

Luke pursed his lips. He could not believe that. There was more rock piled up in that shaft than was likely with the roof simply caving in. Also there were cracks all around in the surface rock. To him, it seemed more like an explosion.

'Who was there with ya, Billy' he asked softly. 'You have a partner there?' Web stared, eyes suddenly wild. 'Yeah, there was somebody . . . Don't rightly remember. This guy . . .'

'Give me a name, Billy. Try to remember.'

59

Web sighed and shook his head. His hands gripped the blanket.

'I don't know. Maybe there was nobody.'

Luke nodded silently. He remembered the bare campsite, stripped of all sign of human occupation. There had been someone there with Billy. That was for sure – a mining-partner who had just left with all speed as soon as the roof of the mine collapsed. Why had he not gone into Smoky Hill to fetch help?

Well, maybe this feller had just decided to avoid all the difficulties and suspicions that would arise from an investigation into a fatal accident. It was irresponsible and cowardly but human nature. Nevertheless, there was no real excuse. Nobody had the right to ride off and leave a man under a pile of rubble in a mine-shaft however little chance there might be of the victim still being alive. As things had turned out Billy had survived, but no thanks to his mining-partner!

A few days later Web was on his feet and becoming increasingly agitated about getting back to Oakfield. Luke had discovered from the stage-driver where the town was and knew it would be a hard journey in winter. Luke reminded Web also that there were not enough horses. If there had been any horses at the mine they had vanished along with the man who had cleared up the camp.

Back at the stables Bitty looked up from grooming a horse and walked slowly over to where Luke and Catfish were conversing in low tones.

'Tell you what,' he said hoarsely, looking at the sawdust-covered floor as he spoke, 'I kin see thet you two fellers want desperate bad to help thet sick man thet you pulled out of the hole and you reckon thet the way to do it is to git him back to Oakfield where he comes from. When you git around to it, I'll buy the horse to carry him there. You remember thet!'

'You?' asked Luke incredulously. 'You can buy the extra horse?'

'Sure. I've been saving up what I could over the years thet I've worked in this here dung-pit and I have enough. You and Catfish are the only two folks thet I could ever count as friends, so you're welcome.'

Luke thanked him while Catfish stared in surprise. Privately, Luke made up his mind that if the journey *was* ever made, Bitty would have his horse back at the end of it. It was a loan. That was all. Bitty was still a poor man whatever he had managed to save from his meagre wages over the years.

Making the trip seemed out of the question anyway as the weather wasn't getting any better. He said as much to Web, who seemed overcome with despair and paced up and down in the shack between bouts of staring out at the snow. At length, he turned to face Luke, his features distorted in a strange mixture of emotions.

'I remember something else, Luke,' he hissed, biting his lips, 'There was this other feller, right enough. His name was Jed, or something like that. I was looking for his watch. That's why I stayed back in the mine in the dark.'

'This feller, Jed, what else do ya remember about him?'

'Nothing. We was just mining, as far as I know. Maybe his name wasn't Jed. Maybe it was Billy, or something.'

'You're Billy,' Luke reminded him.

'Yeah,' answered Web uncertainly.

'There must be something you remember about your partner, Billy. What did he look like? Was he older than you or was he a young kind of guy? What did he look like? Where did ya meet him? Did the pair of you find gold in thet old mine?' Maybe that had been a reason for something that had happened. Perhaps the gold had gone off in the saddle-bags of the horses that should have been on that campsite but had gone without trace. 'Try to remember something more, Billy.'

'I can't!' yelled Web suddenly, covering his face with his hands.

'All right, Billy,' said Luke quietly, realizing he had questioned too hard.

Nevertheless, Luke felt sure that his suspicions regarding the missing miner were correct. That explosion had been no accident. Billy, or whatever his name was, was a dead man in the mind of the guy who had ridden calmly away from that campsite. There was a reason for the whole thing. It had something to do with money – the money that belonged by rights to the corpse supposedly buried under the rubble.

Luke was more determined than ever to solve the mystery and to help this mentally sick man who had escaped death by such a narrow margin. He worried about it over the days that followed while the snow swept in anew. His mind had been on the sick man's problems for about two weeks and, unbeknown to himself, his own heart had lightened as he had thought less of his own situation and unpleasant memories of his past life faded as a result. Helping the sick had become the main thing in his life during the war and somehow it meant as much now as it did then.

The weather cleared after a few more days and early one morning Catfish stood outside his shack gazing over the wide expanse of glittering snow. There came a faraway look in his eyes and it was still there as he went back indoors for some minutes and argued with his wife, who had just finished serving up breakfast to the sick white man. When he came out he mounted his pony with unaccustomed alacrity and rode as fast as was possible into town.

'I got something to say,' he remarked to Luke. 'I ain't done nothin' worth a damn since I came here an' I've had about enough of it. When I was young I was a hunter and a warrior but now I'm nothin' but a horse-scrubber. Thing is, I know a way through this snow that will take us north to this goddamned place that the crazy man wants to git to. I kin lead, like I used to when I was scout for the Army an' even before thet when I led Iron Bull and his braves along thet trail to wipe out the Striped Feathered Arrows – although we got the worst of it in the end because there were more of them than we figured.'

'You fought against the Cheyenne?' asked Luke, interested.

'Sure. The Dakota always did fight them. But thet ain't what I'm getting at. There's a valley thet goes through the hills. It's narrow and twists like a snake. We used to call it the Snake. It hardly ever gits filled up with snow. It'll be about clear now. It's the only way if you want to move before spring.'

He looked at Luke expectantly, his old eyes eager, nostrils expanding with a hint of excitement. Luke stared as the idea turned over in his mind. He had confidence in old Catfish. The Indian was not a man to make such a claim if he was not sure of his ground.

'All right,' he answered at length. 'We'll hit that trail.'

Two days later they were on their way. Bitty provided money for the much-needed horse and, to their surprise, insisted upon coming too. They wore their warmest clothing and between them Luke and Bitty bought in enough food for the journey. They also provided enough food for Mary Elk to see her through the likely period of her husband's absence. She raved and cried when it became clear to her that Catfish was going but he was adamant and there was nothing she could do about it.

Fortunately the weather kept clear on the day they set off. The snow was crisp underfoot and the horses made reasonable time for winter travel. The party moved at no more than a walking-pace through the white expanse and continued throughout the daylight hours. It was better to keep moving than to attempt to hurry on and then to be forced to stop for rest in the cold.

Nevertheless, as Luke saw the weak winter sun descending he knew they must call a halt soon. He worried much about that for it would be a dangerous matter to be caught out in the open if a storm blew up.

'Place 'way up on trail!' Catfish suddenly called. He was taking his turn as leader, breaking the ground for the other horses, while his own mount at the moment was up to its shoulders in an unexpected drift. 'Reckon we need to stop there. Thet's what I think!'

Catfish was full of a new-found confidence. It was as if he had left his years as a nobody behind him in Smoky Hill and had stepped back into a time when he had lived a life of travel and danger. His shoulders had straightened up and he held his head high.

'We'll give it a try!' shouted Luke in agreement. He could see the tiny shack a long way ahead, dark against the snow. He knew it was the only place they could find shelter before nightfall and he was determined not to pass it by, regardless of who owned it or who might be staying there.

As it turned out there was no one in the rough building. It had obviously been abandoned years before. One wall was caved in and the roof was in danger of collapsing under the weight of snow. But it provided shelter for men and horses and they were all delighted to take advantage of it. A fire was lit from timbers of the collapsed wall and the night was made tolerable.

Towards next evening they had come a long way and were beginning to climb slowly up the foothills. The weather, however, was looking worse, with a rising wind and scattering snow. Darkness brought no abandoned shack to comfort them and they could do no more than huddle in the lee of a boulder-strewn ridge. Luke insisted upon covering the horses with the heaviest blankets while he and his men did with less. If even one animal succumbed to the cold it would be the end of the trip and likely enough the end of them too.

About the middle of the next afternoon Catfish pointed ahead at a rocky peak just visible through the driving snow.

'Thet's it!' he yelled, voice drifting away in the wind. 'Scalplock Stone! It's jest about there Snake takes over!'

'Thet's Thompson Butte, ain't it?' objected Bitty, having heard something of it before.

'Scalplock, fer Chrisake!' growled Catfish. 'It sure is Scalplock! What the hell you mean giving it some crazy white man name?'

Whatever anybody cared to call it, the sharp peak had at its foot a ravine, shallow and snow-covered at first, which became narrower as they rode into it with the snow underfoot gradually petering out. Overhead, the sides of the ravine seemed to climb to meet the sky so that only a thin line of light could be seen. The prevailing wind carried its burden of snow swiftly from one sharp edge to the other and little fell to meet the flat, dried-up watercourse that had found its way through the earthquake-splintered rock of a bygone age.

There was no wind and comparatively little cold. Luke and Catfish and Bitty smiled at one another in relief. Catfish seemed puffed up with pride when Luke congratulated him on his superior knowledge and experience. Only Web was silent, his mind falling once again into the pit from which he had been rescued. The high rocky walls seemed to weigh down upon him, and his spirits, which had seemed a little uplifted on the previous days, plunged again to new depths.

'It's, all right, Billy,' said Luke, understanding. 'We'll soon get to Oakfield.'

An exhausting week had to pass, though, before he could fulfil his promise. They made good time through the Snake but even so, it was hard going. The ground was rough and strewn with boulders and they had to camp throughout the bitter nights without shelter. It was with some sense of relief that they eventually left the canyon behind and rode out into the white expanse of open country, knowing that their journey must be almost over.

The white glare stretched for miles ahead with nothing to break its monotony but the far of gleam of the river, not looking frozen as yet but with a glittering hint of ice at its margins. There was still a long way to go but it was mostly down-hill and it seemed to Luke that the weather might hold for the rest of the day.

He was wrong in that, for the wind rose in the late afternoon and brought with it a light snow that threatened to become a storm very quickly. Before the view ahead was obscured, however, they made out the dark shape of a building a mile or so to the north-west.

They turned in that direction and hoped desperately that they would not wander past it as the snowfall grew heavier. Luck was with them and after a long, wearisome and almost blind struggle they were within reach of it. Catfish called out that he could see as plain as Mary Elk's nose at the window.

It was not much of a place as far as could be seen but to them it seemed an answer to their prayers. They passed a fence, almost buried under snow, and then two rough wooden buildings, one obviously a stable, but the other a human habitation. There was a light in the doorway and a smell of wood-smoke in the air.

Luke dismounted first and shouted so that the owner of the property would not be suddenly alarmed at the party's appearing at the door. There was a long hesitation, then a glare of lamplight at the window. A moment later and the end of a rifle barrel projected from behind the doorpost.

'Hold it right there!' came a shouted command. 'Another step and you git a bullet in the guts!'

'We're travelling, mister,' answered Luke pacifically. 'It's all right. We ain't looking for trouble. We have enough! All we want is shelter for the night.'

He could understand the man's suspicions. A group of four horsemen coming out of nowhere at an isolated homestead was likely enough to be met by a raised rifle.

They waited in the bitter cold wind while the

man inside made up his mind. He did not seem to be in a hurry but when he spoke again there was no hint of alarm in his voice but neither was there any trace of friendliness.

'Any of you guys armed?'

'I have a sidegun,' said Luke, 'but, as I say, we're jest needing somewhere to shelter for the night. We kin pay too.'

'Fine!' The voice held the hint of a sarcastic chuckle but it seemed that the man's misgivings had vanished. 'Come on in. You kin leave the horses over there in the stable, only I hope you have animal feed with you because there ain't much here.'

They put the horses into shelter as a matter of priority and gave them a hefty portion of feed from the saddle-bags. The cold was eating into Luke's hands as they saw to their mounts but, like Catfish and Bitty, he had been working too long with horses to put his own comfort first.

The door of the shack was open and for the first time Luke saw their host. He was tall and well-built with dark hair, cut much shorter than was usual. He was also clean-shaven and handsome in a rugged way, but the lamplight showed a lean face heavily pockmarked from some past disease. His grin revealed that he had lost two teeth. It also suggested a personality more accustomed to sneering than to smiling.

All those facts Luke observed within a second. He also noted that the man wore an army tunic and boots and carried a Navy pistol at his belt.

'My name's Luke Coyle.' Luke tried to sound friendly but did not find that easy when faced with this man. 'These are my friends, Bitty, Billy and Catfish. As I say, we jest need shelter for the night, then we'll be on our way.'

'I'm Major Heston, late of the United States Cavalry,' came the reply. It sounded almost like a boast. Somehow, Luke felt it was not true, but he smiled through his snow-covered lips anyway, fully aware of the need to get along with the fellow.

'All right,' Heston was peering out into the shadows as he held up his lamp and caught sight of Catfish, 'but I don't take no Injuns. He'll have to sleep in the stable.'

Luke felt his anger rising. Such an attitude towards Indians was not so very uncommon but he found it unacceptable. Indians in general were no worse than the average white person. Some had even fought in the war alongside the white troops.

'Catfish is a friend of mine,' he said quietly. 'He's one of us. If he goes to the stable so do I.'

Heston stared at him, a glimmer of contempt

that changed rapidly to anger coming into his pale eyes.

'I'm offering you my hospitality, mister,' he answered in a low tone that held a hint of menace. 'You refusing it?'

Luke could see that Heston was a man with a short temper. In other circumstances he would have walked back out through the open door but there was nowhere to go in this snowstorm. For a moment, he was not certain how to reply but then Catfish, himself, intervened.

'It's all right, Luke,' he grunted. 'I kin sleep in the stable. Horses make as good company as some humans.'

Heston's rifle lifted a couple of inches.

'Don't get smart, Injun,' he hissed, 'or you'll be on your way out into the snow or maybe to hell.'

'Leave it!' snapped Luke. He knew he could not afford to quarrel with Heston. 'Have it your own way. Catfish, you make sure you have plenty of blankets. We'll bring you hot coffee and food. Soon as it's ready.'

Luke's eyes met those of Heston. It was as if gunsmoke hung in the air.

5

The interior of the shack was warm from the hot wood-burning stove. It contained some rough furniture and an old mat on the floor. There was a table with a plate and a metal mug and a knife, all recently used. A faint trace of coffee still lingered in the air.

It was just about as Luke had expected, except for the walls. They were hung with a variety of weapons – rifles, carbines, an old musket, and sidearms too. Luke recognized an Enfield rifle musket, Spencer and Henry rifles, a Remington Whitney revolver and a Colt Navy, all much used in the Civil War. There were also a couple of sabres, hanging crossed above the door, and a shining bayonet near the stove.

Heston saw Luke stare and grinned with a hint of satisfaction. His anger seemed to have

subsided for the moment, since he had
succeeded in packing the Indian off to the
stable.

'I was all through the war,' he remarked. 'I
guess you can see that. Most of this stuff I picked
up from the battlefields. I was at Bull Run and
Gettysburg and Chickamauga and a hell of a lot
of other places too! You fellers in the war?'

'Me . . . I was in it,' replied Luke with obvious
lack of interest. 'My friends here didn't get
caught up in it.'

Heston glanced at Bitty and Web, frowning as
he looked at the latter. 'This guy all right?' he
asked. 'Looks as if his brain's in the moon or
someplace.'

'He's tired,' explained Luke. 'We all are. We
could do with warm food and a hot drink.'

'It's on its way,' growled Heston. 'What the
hell you think this is – the Grand Hotel in
Oakfield or what? Anyhow, jest remember that
what you eat, you pay for!'

'We know it,' answered Luke.

Heston persisted in talking about the war as
they ate and drank. It seemed to be an obsession
with him.

'What did you do?' he asked Luke pointedly.
'See much action?'

'In the field hospitals mostly – plenty of

wounded and dying.'

'I guess I sent a good many there,' chuckled Heston. 'That is, to the Reb hospital and to their graves too. Made quite a gap in the Confederate front line with my sharpshooting. Hell of a time!'

'It's over with,' sighed Luke.

'Yeah, but I keep up with my shooting. That's a skill I kin never lose! Fast as hell on the draw now, I kin tell you! Brought down an eagle with my Colt last summer as it flew over this house. Kin you believe thet? With a Colt!'

'Why?'asked Luke.

'What do ya mean?'

'Why shoot the eagle?'

'What kind of a question is that? You got buffalo-chips in the head, or somethin'?'

Shortly afterwards they went to sleep in the other small room where they lay on the floor all night. Luke did not rest easy, knowing that Heston was just on the other side of the wall wrapped in a blanket by the stove. He could not trust the man. There was no real danger as Heston had nothing to gain by any act of treachery, but Luke's hand remained on his own side-gun in the darkness.

Next morning they left as quickly as possible and made good time as the weather had eased.

By mid-afternoon they were in sight of the smoke rising from the chimneys of Oakfield in the distance. They entered the outskirts just before dusk fell and made their way up the main street, looking for somewhere to stay the night.

They found the Low Dog saloon, which was shabby and run-down but looked inexpensive. The owner had a couple of rooms round the back that he was in the habit of renting out to travellers like themselves and he did not mind taking in a civilized Indian as long as he could pay his way. They ate better than they had on the previous evening and slept the sleep of exhaustion. Luke did not stir until the very early hours before dawn when he lay in the dark and wondered about the place called Goldcrest and how Billy – if that was really his name – fitted into it. . . .

Some time after the wintry sun arose on that same day, Jed Parker was ready to take to the trail. He planned to ride into Oakfield because he was desperately short of money and believed he could persuade the bank to advance him a substantial loan on the strength of his position as a prosperous rancher with mining interests. The hundred dollars he had found in Eric Webster's desk had been whittled away and now he was down to the few bucks he had in his waistcoat-pocket.

He was a little surprised to find Gus standing outside with the horse already saddled.

'You said ya were goin' into town, this morning, Mr Webster, so I reckoned it would be a help to git the animal ready.'

'Hey, that was good of you!' said Parker. 'You're a real help all round!'

'Thing is, Mr Webster, I wondered if I could have a few words with ya?'

'Jest now?'

'Yeah, if you kin spare the time. . . . The thing is, your brother, Mr Eric, always said as how he thought a hell of a lot of me an' my brother, Crow. He always reckoned we could be top hands and was jest about to fix us up like thet when he took ill and had to run down the place until he got better. Only, of course, he never did, which was a hell of a thing, him dying, which we're sure all real cast down about, although we're sure as hell glad to have you here! Anyway, he had promised to make Crow a kind of fore-man over the stockmen, which Crow sure could do, no trouble, and Mr Eric said too thet I could handle the top job as a manager over the whole thing, always working under his instructions, of course, which he was sure I could do as well, no trouble. So we thought, Crow and me thet is, thet after you git things fixed up here, you would want to carry out Mr Eric's wishes and take us on as your top men.'

Gus stopped as if to gather his breath and seemed to stare at the snow at his feet although he looked at Parker under one raised eyebrow.

Parker gazed at him without expression. He saw now what he had only suspected before – all the helpfulness, the consideration, the ingratiating manner had to do with Gus's need to get something for himself out of this new situation. He wanted to benefit from the change that had taken place at Goldcrest.

Parker did not believe that Eric Webster had ever offered positions of responsibility to Gus and Crow. They were not the kind of men that could be trusted to do well at anything except fairly menial tasks such as grooming horses or mending fences. All this talk about Eric Webster looking to give them promotion in his running of Goldcrest did not amount to anything but lies.

Not that Parker was greatly surprised to find himself being lied to. It was the way in which he tended to think himself. He had lived much of his own life by telling one lie after another whenever it seemed like a good idea. To find that Gus and his brother Crow had such a low, venal attitude fitted in to his own way of thinking much better than the notion that they were naturally kindly and obliging.

He reflected for only a second in deciding how to react to Gus's little speech. He would play along with them for the time being. He needed their full co-operation right now, and maybe for some time to come. Later he would deal with them as he saw fit.

'That's absolutely right, Gus,' he enthused. 'Eric was a smart man! There's no doubt that you're the kind of men that a ranch-owner can have faith in. I'll see you both all right, believe me!'

He rode away, leaving Gus with a twisted smile on his rugged features. As he rode through the snow he soon forgot the conversation and turned his mind fully to his forthcoming interview with the bank manager. He needed to play his own part with a show of real confidence and an appearance of utter sincerity. He had little doubt about that. As a hypocrite, he was a million miles ahead of Gus and Crow.

As it turned out the meeting went perfectly and, after a short business discussion and the signing of a few papers, all was well. Parker slipped a package containing $5,000 in bills into his pocket. The bank manager regarded it as a good deal too, as the interest to be charged was high enough to bring in a good profit.

So Parker stepped out of the bank with a smile on his face and stood for a moment in the pale sunlight, feeling that the world was really opening up in front of him and everything was going to go his way from now on.

Then he turned on the sidewalk towards his horse, which he had left hitched to the railing. To his surprise he saw the figure of a man standing there with a hand on the animal's neck. The man was wearing a heavy checked jacket of the kind worn by lumbermen, warm but very shabby in appearance, as if he had bought it second-hand.

Nearby there stood another man, a young feller with long fair hair and the bulge of a side-gun under his dark jacket. He was staring at the man by the horse with a quizzical expression, as if he was listening intently to what was being said.

'Billy,' said the man in the lumber jacket. 'This is my Billy. Sure as guns.'

Parker stood as though transfixed. The voice was that of Web – the man whose voice ought to have been stilled for ever under the pile of rock in the old gold-mine. . . .

For a moment Parker could not move. Only

his face changed. The expression of self-satisfaction vanished and was replaced by astonishment and horror. His eyes bulged and his mouth twisted as if he sought to speak but could not do so.

'What do you mean?' The young feller with the fair hair spoke to the man in the lumber jacket. 'Is your own name *not* Billy?'

'Nope, this here's Billy.'

The man by the horse turned round and Parker looked into the face of Harry Webster.

There was silence. Harry stared at Parker as if in half-recognition. His mouth moved but without utterance. The fair-haired man looked too, eyes widening a little as he seemed to take in Parker's expression. Parker gulped and tried to pull himself together.

'What do you want with my horse?' he asked, forcing a little indignation into his tone to cover up his sudden fear. He moved forward and put his hand on the bridle, thrusting Harry slightly to the side. 'His name ain't Billy.'

'What's his name then?' asked Luke suddenly, his tone full of suspicion.

'Name?' Parker's imagination seemed to desert him. 'Nothin'. He don't have a name. He's just a goddamned horse. Thet's all!'

He found himself looking straight into Harry's

eyes at close quarters. They held a bewildered expression. It was evident to Parker that his former gold-mining partner did not quite recognize him. He looked ill too, as if he had not recovered from the explosion in the mine. Nevertheless, there was something going on at the back of his eyes as if he sought desperately to remember.

'You all right, Mr Webster?' The bank guard stood at the door, shotgun slightly raised. The man was staring at the little group of strangers which had grown to four as he watched, all of them looking like low-down drifters and with an Indian amongst them. 'No trouble, I hope, Mr Webster?'

'No, it's all right,' answered Parker thickly as he mounted his horse. 'Jest a mistake of some kind, I reckon.'

He left town as fast as his horse would take him through the slush of the streets. His mind was in turmoil as he took the snow-covered trail back to the ranch. Harry Webster's return was like a ghost appearing at his bedside. His heart thumped and he cursed wildly under his breath. As he had stared into Harry's eyes it was as if a knife had been raised to deal him a death-blow.

Gradually, as he extended the distance between himself and Oakfield, he got his nerves under control, but he did not know what to do. It was obvious that Harry's mind was impaired after the trauma of his narrow escape but it might not remain so. If and when he remembered, things would go badly with his, Parker's, plans and he would very shortly be on the wrong side of the law as his treachery and theft and attempted murder were all revealed.

When he reached the house Parker locked the front door as if he expected an attack. It was senseless, as he knew, but he needed to shut out the world until he found time to think.

That night and the following day went by in a storm of driving wind and sleet. Parker saw no one except Crow, who came to stable the horse and shouted something unintelligible through the door in answer to which Parker yelled back that he did not want anything and was busy.

As he paced the house in his agitation, Parker racked his brain for a solution but without any satisfactory result. Sometimes he thought, and even willed himself to believe, that Harry would remember no more than the name of that goddamned horse. Those moments of optimism were, however, short-lived as he knew perfectly well that a man who for one reason or another had lost his memory would be very likely to regain it.

In the end he came to the conclusion that had been in the depths of his mind from the moment he had heard Harry Webster's voice outside the bank. He could not allow the man he had left for dead to re-emerge from the grave that had been planned for him. Harry must die for a second time.

He pondered long and hard as to how he might achieve his desire. It would have to be done in such a way that no suspicion was ever levelled at himself. There was no cunning accident that could be arranged, therefore Harry must die as a result of shooting. There was a way of doing that just inside the law – self-defence might be offered as a plea if it could be shown that Harry had tried to kill him, but that was not easy to manage. It would almost certainly have to be *outside* the law. A bullet in the back would be the best answer but it was too risky to attempt that unless the plan was arranged very carefully and the victim led into a trap.

He was unwilling to attempt the murder himself. There was too much in his present life to be risked. In some situations he might have gone ahead with it in the belief that, as a last resort, he could perhaps make his escape on a fast horse, but he had no intention of riding away from his present life. He was a rich man.

He had to stay where he was in order to enjoy the fruits of own selfishness and ruthlessness. He applied those terms to himself in his own mind without hesitation. He was not ashamed of being the kind of man he was. It did not occur to him that most men were not as himself.

Which thought brought him around to Gus and Crow. They were the only men anywhere around Oakfield whom he knew fairly well. He had met few people since arriving at Goldcrest and no one whom he could approach with any plan such as he had in mind. His conversation with Gus a couple of days ago had convinced him that they both looked to him for self-advancement. To what extent they might be prepared to go in pursuit of a rich future he could not tell but he recognized the need to find out.

He rode over to their little farm that same afternoon. On the way, he passed the shack where the girl lived and noted a hint of smoke arising from the chimney. It was weak enough to suggest a dying fire. She might not be at home right now, he thought vaguely. He had heard that she sometimes worked in town. He gave the matter no real consideration, as he had no interest in her.

When he got to Gus's place he was invited in

at once. Both men were very surprised and pleased to see him.

'Hey, come in outa the cold, Mr Webster,' urged Gus. 'Let me take your coat. Sit by the fire. What kin we do for you?'

'Well, I came over to see you fellers for a couple of reasons,' answered Parker in an almost jovial tone as if he had not a care in the world. 'For one thing, I want to give you this . . .' He drew a hundred dollars from his waistcoat pocket and handed them fifty each. 'This is to show my appreciation of everything you're doing around the place. You've shown yourselves to be invaluable.'

Total astonishment registered on their faces, to be replaced immediately by delight. It was far more money than they could ever have expected for the work they had done since his arrival at Goldcrest. Gus opened and shut his mouth as if unable to speak. Crow's eyes seemed to mist over.

After a moment or two they expressed their gratitude, struggling to find the words. Parker waved their thanks aside with a grand gesture.

'It's all right, fellers, you deserve every cent of it. My brother was right in his assessment of you both. You're first class, no doubt about it! Which brings me on to your future with me. I've been thinking, Gus, about what you were sayin' the other day, and it seems clear that I couldn't do better than to give you the position here that my brother, Eric, was planning for you. And the same goes for Crow. Stick with me and you won't regret it. Us three will build a future together that'll be like a dream come true.'

He paused to watch the impression made upon them by his words, which was, as he expected, incredulity mixed with immense pride. They were like a couple of not very bright soldiers who had just had a medal pinned on them by the general.He then allowed his eyes to sink to the floor and his shoulders to droop as if he could no longer contain the heaviness of some internal burden.

'Somethin' wrong, Mr Webster?' asked Gus with concern.

'Well, the thing is,' sighed Parker, 'I've got bad trouble . . .' He permitted his voice to trail off and waited a full minute before continuing. 'I wondered if you fellers could help me?' He looked straight at them, seeming to bore into their eyes. 'Either of you two been in the war?'

'Nope,' answered Gus, in a whisper, suddenly overawed by Parker's tragic demeanour. 'We were both kind of older than most of the guys that went.'

'So you ain't seen much action. I mean fight-ing. Can you use guns?'

'Sure, we kin do thet!' Gus brightened, glad to be able to show himself in a better light. 'In the old days, when things were pretty rough, we learnt to handle ourselves. Had to or we would-n't be here now! Thet right, Crow?'

'You got it,' growled Crow. 'Only way to stay alive in them days.'

'Ever kill anybody?' asked Parker bluntly.

'Well, yeah, we were in plenty of gunfights. I reckon I put paid to a couple of guys. It was them or me. Same with Crow. He downed some too. We wouldn't be here now if we hadn't!'

'I know it,' said Parker approvingly. 'A man needs to defend himself. Only it kin catch up with him, years later. . . .' He looked at the floor and then looked again at them both as if attempting to look into their hearts. 'Let me tell you somethin', fellers, let me be straight with you; I killed a man years ago. It was a straight gun-to-gun fight, jest like you been talking about, and he got the worst of it, which is what he had been asking for. The law didn't get mixed up in it because in them days there wasn't much law around. But it's all coming back.' He spread his hands as he continued with his lies, as if to show that there was no way he wished to hide any of the truth from them. 'He had a friend, this guy, a ruthless no-good killer like himself. He vowed to git even with me. It didn't happen at the time but now he's come back.'

Gus and Crow sat up straight, faces drawn in concern.

'I saw him the other day in Oakfield,' went on Parker, 'and he has men with him. He's out to git me. He told me to my face. That's where I need your help.'

Gus stared in amazement and then cast his eyes to the floor.

'What about the law, Mr Webster? You should git the sheriff into this. It ain't somethin' ya need to do on your own.'

He meant that he did not relish getting mixed up in the matter. Parker could read that much in his answer.

'How kin I do thet?' asked Parker appealingly. 'It would all come out about thet killing I was forced to do all them years ago and . . .' He searched quickly for another lie and found it, 'there was another thing too. I was guilty of theft at the time, I gotta admit it. You see, after I left my brother, things went pretty bad for me. I got into wrong company. You know how it is! Me and the guy I eventually killed were mixed up in a bank robbery. This feller who's after me now knows about it. It would all come out, sure as guns, then where would I be – in jail! Goldcrest would be deserted. I would be finished and – I hate to say this, fellers – but you would be too. You wouldn't even be able to stay in this here shack!'

He paused to see the effect of his words and was pleased to note the shock in their expressions.

'We got to take the bull by the horns, Gus,' he went on. 'To sit and do nothing is suicide. We need to fix this guy and his men ourselves. We kin do it too, if we're smart enough and keep our nerve and ain't afraid of killing a few rats!'

'How?' asked Gus, after a pause. The fact that Parker had just admitted being a bank robber did not concern him. He had not always been strictly honest himself. 'How kin we do it?'

'We'll draw them into a trap. Make it look like they were out to rob Goldcrest and had to be dealt with jest like the bunch of outlaws they are! They look like the orneriest bunch you ever set eyes on, anyhow. Easy for any sheriff to believe he's looking at the shot-dead remains of no-account drifters and saddle tramps.'

'I kin see what ya mean in all this, Mr Webster,' said Gus. 'Looks like we ain't got much of a choice. Only the thing is thet Crow and me ain't done any serious shooting in a long time.'

'It's all for all of our futures,' insisted Parker. 'We need to give it everything we've got. If we surprise them they kin be shot down afore they kin draw at all.'

Gus looked at Crow who was staring at Parker as though mesmerized. Then Gus's face brightened just a little.

'Tell ya what, Mr Webster,' he said. 'We'll help all we kin. We kin shoot straight enough if we're kind of close to what we're shooting at. Like you say, if this gang ain't expecting it an' we ain't being looked at by the law or anybody, then we kin shoot them down like sick cattle, but I reckon it would be better if we had some real good help.'

'Yeah, what do you mean?' enquired Parker.

'Major Heston. He's the man for this, I reckon.'

6

In the dingy little room in the Low Dog saloon Luke questioned 'Billy' slowly and carefully in an attempt to jog his memory. The reaction of the rancher on the sidewalk outside the bank struck him as being very strange. He was also certain that Billy was in fact the name of the horse that had been hitched to the railing there. No man would give his horse the same name as himself nor was it likely that a horse used for daily riding would have no name. It was not the way folks thought about horses. There was a mistake and a lie mixed up in this situation and he needed to find out the truth.

It was not an easy task. The sick man seemed under a greater strain than ever and there were times when he did not answer at all. When he spoke, he continued to insist that the horse was called Billy, but that was all.

In the end Luke came to the conclusion that he had to speak to the man who had come out of the bank. He remembered that the bank guard had referred to him as Mr Webster. After walking thoughtfully outside Luke went back to the little room. He sat deliberately in front of the sick man and stared straight at him as he spoke.

'Goldcrest is the name of the ranch and there's a man called Webster. What's the connection?'

'Goldcrest? Thet's where I need to git to. Thet's it!' yelled Web. It was the first time he had mentioned the ranch since journeying through the Snake ravine. His eyes were widening.

'What's your name?' shouted Luke suddenly, feeling that a door might be opening.

'Web! Thet's it – my name's Web!'

That was all but it seemed very significant. Web – short for Webster! Luke had no doubt now that he must talk to the man he had seen that day. He made up his mind to ride out to Goldcrest. The weather worsened, however, and by late afternoon a fierce storm of sleet began which went on through the night and throughout the next day. Travel was impossible so they had to content themselves by staying in the saloon. They ate meagrely because funds were running low, to the silent irritation of the proprietor who regarded them as pretty poor customers and a rough-looking lot at that, their only saving grace being that they did not seem to be looking for trouble and only the young feller was armed.

In the morning the weather cleared and they walked out into the cold air, glad to fill their lungs. Luke still had it in mind to get to the ranch that day if at all possible, as he believed that a conversation with the man they had met outside the bank might help to clear up the mystery that Web's amnesia still persisted in concealing.

They had not gone many steps along the main street, however, when they found themselves face to face with a young woman. She was dressed in a dark coat and hood and a lock of black hair straggled across her forehead. Luke was about to step from the sidewalk to allow her to pass when the fleeting expression of irritation that had been in her face changed to surprise.

She was staring straight at Web who had stopped in his tracks as though thunderstruck. Neither said a word for a full minute and Luke had time to see that her grey eyes, her cheekbones and the shape of her mouth were all reflected in the features of Web. . . .

'Pardon us, ma'am,' said Luke, his mind beginning to jump with questions. 'We seem to have got in your way. Let me introduce my friends, Web, Catfish and Bitty. I'm Luke Coyle.' Normally he would never have thought of speaking to a lady he had never met in such a way but something about the situation seemed to call for it. 'I think Web, here, may really carry the name Webster, by rights.'

She ignored Luke's remarks as she would have ignored any stranger who had the nerve to speak to her in the street but stared at Web as though hypnotized. Web stared back. Luke waited for one of them to speak but to no avail.

'Web, here,' he said pointedly, 'has been in an accident. He can't remember much right now. Have you met him before?'

His question seemed to break the spell and she glanced at him as if seeing him for the first time. She shook her head and made to hurry on before changing her mind and turning back to the group.

'Where do you come from?' she asked Luke. He told her Smoky Hill and then that they were on their way to the ranch called Goldcrest. Her face registered her amazement.

'You say your friend here has lost his memory?'

'Thet's it,' answered Luke, pleased at her sudden interest. 'He was in a mining accident . . . a gold-mine. But he reckons he has business at Goldcrest. He remembers thet much.'

The mention of Goldcrest struck a cord. She said nothing but looked from one to the other of the shabby group of men. Luke knew she was embarrassed. It was not the thing for a young lady to be seen talking in the street to a bunch of rough strangers. He knew she wanted to continue but there was nowhere to go. No respectable woman could go into the saloon.

'Maybe we could talk out of town, ma'am,' he suggested, as if he had read her mind.

'All right,' she said with sudden decision. 'Ride out by the west side of the town. I'll be at the old elm tree. It's about two miles from here. In an hour.'

They obeyed her instructions and rode out into the white expanse on the west side of the town. In the distance they caught sight of a saddleback hill, snow-covered against the sky.

'Hey!' called Web in sudden excitement, 'way up there ya kin find old Indian mounds like as if they used to bury their dead there in the old days!'

'Yeah,' put in Catfish. 'Thet was the old people long afore them pesky Whites ever came to them parts!'

Luke grinned, mostly because he felt delighted that Web could remember something more, however inconsequential.

'Tell you somethin', Catfish and Bitty,' he said after a moment's thought, 'I reckon it might be better if you two rode back to town. The gal won't really like to be meeting a whole bunch of guys like us.'

The elm was easy to find. The girl came riding over the snow from another direction. As she approached, Luke again noted how pretty she was – like an early flower in the snow, he thought, a tiny smile twitching the corners of his mouth.

But she did not smile back and he noted that she had been careful enough to carry a revolver at her saddle. He respected her all the more for that. She listened as he told her everything he knew about Web and his accident and the old gold-mine and Catfish and Bitty and the man called Webster outside the bank. When he had finished, she made no reply except for a brief word of thanks. Then, to his surprise, she turned to ride away.

'You going back to Oakfield, ma'am,' he asked impulsively.

'No – to Goldcrest, she answered. 'By the way,

my name's Spence – Jenny Spence.'

He watched her until she was out of sight, her white pony seeming to vanish beneath her against the snow. Web watched her go too. He had not been able to take his eyes off her at all during the meeting. Suddenly he shouted out: 'Anne!' but the girl was already well out of earshot. Luke stared at him in astonishment. The girl had said her name was Jenny.

At just about the same time as the meeting with the girl in the snow was taking place Gus was riding to the cabin of the man who called himself Major Heston. It was a long ride through the snow and he was glad enough to get there so that he could rest, although he had no liking for Heston and did not look forward to carrying out the task that he had brought upon himself by his advice to Parker.

Heston opened the cabin door, rifle in hand, and glared at Gus suspiciously. Nevertheless, after listening to Parker's proposition, he invited Gus over the threshold and offered him a warm drink, which was gratefully accepted.

'So Webster wants to settle things with these guys? Must be pretty important to him. He must have somethin' to hide too, eh? Wants to keep clear of the sheriff!' He laughed sardonically. 'Well, I kin jest about understand thet! What about these fellers? He say what they were like?'

Gus described the rough gang of saddle tramps as he had heard it from Parker and Heston suddenly hooted with laughter.

'Jeeze! An Indian and a young feller with long hair and a couple of old guys! I know *them*, fer Christ's sake! They was here!' He looked at Gus in amazement. 'What the hell's wrong with Webster thet he can't do this on his own?'

Gus shrugged and drank the rest of his coffee in a gulp. 'Jest his way.'

Gus returned to Goldcrest armed with Heston's agreement to come and talk things over with Webster. There was, of course, the matter of payment, which was unlikely to be modest, especially as Heston had guessed that the request for help had been prompted by a good measure of desperation.

After Gus had gone Heston sat deep in thought for some time and then rode over the snow to a dilapidated shack about a mile from his own. There he roused out of their beds four out-of-work cowhands, two of them half-Indian, and all of them smelling of drink and stale sweat. They were low, foul men, generally idle but ready to do anything for money. They were willing to turn their hands to any task so long as it did not require hard work. Violence had long been a speciality of theirs, always carried out without finesse and with no thought of mercy.

Parker saw Heston and his men coming late that same afternoon as he stood at the window of his upstairs bedroom. He jumped with uneasiness as they drew nearer and he was able to make out details of their rough appearance. Gus had already informed him of Heston's willingness to help but he had not expected a gang of ruffians.

He went down to his front porch to receive them and noted with some slight relief that Heston ordered his followers to come to a halt about a hundred yards from the house.

'Thought you and me should talk in private to start with, Webster,' grinned Heston, from a comfortable armchair. 'Them guys . . .' he jerked his head back to the silent group with a hint of contempt, 'are useful in their own way and will make things easier since you have *four* fellers to deal with.' He looked carefully at Parker as if trying to read his mind. 'What kind of a problem do ya have?'

Parker repeated the story he had given to Gus and Crow but was uncertain that he was believed. Heston's face betrayed no expression except a faint hint of contempt. The truth was he reckoned Parker's tale about the old-time duel and the loser's friend looking for revenge was pretty far-fetched. Parker, he felt sure, had some other reason for wanting this gang of saddle tramps silenced. Whatever it was, Heston made up his mind to find out and then to make the rich rancher pay through the nose for the help he was given and for the secret to be kept.

'There's the matter of pay,' said Heston, grinning. 'Jobs like this don't come cheap. Five thousand dollars.'

Parker gasped. It would clean him out. All the money he had just borrowed from the bank would go on this!

'That's a hefty payment! What about. . . ?'

'Forget it,' snapped Heston, making as if to rise.

'All right,' said Parker hastily. 'Two thousand before the job and the rest after.'

'Agreed,' answered Heston, as if making a concession. 'But make sure the cash is all there with no mistake. I ain't a patient man. You got some kind of a plan in all this?'

'Yeah. I have to make it look as if I am well-justified in the eyes of the law for killing even a bunch of drifters like them, so it's to look as if they came here to attack and rob me. I'm going to get them to come to the ranch in a bunch and then they kin be shot down. Thet's where you come in. I reckoned I needed your expertise along with Crow's and Gus's, but I didn't ask for anybody else . . .' He pointed out of the window in the direction of Heston's followers. 'I reckon we don't need every goddamned hill-billy with a gun and a grudge in the county!'

'Save it!' laughed Heston. 'These fellers won't cause no trouble and I'll take care of their wages. I reckon that they're better killers than Crow and Gus kin ever be. You need reliable men in a situation like this, not squeamish farmers who don't like killing a chicken on its birthday! Anyhow, what's your plan for getting these guys to come up here?'

'They have a problem about this ranch thet they want to sort out. Right now, the young feller who looks like the leader has an open mind on the whole thing. I'll send a message to come here to meet my lawyer to talk things over. But there won't be no lawyer. Jest bullets and then a report to the sheriff about a vicious attack from a gang of no-good gunslingers. Thet's when you and your friends will need to make yourselves scarce. It needs to look like self-defence, not a massacre!'

Heston laughed.

'Gunslingers! These guys only have one gun between the lot of them! You don't know thet? I do because I gave them board and lodgings a couple of nights ago. Unless they've bought guns in Oakfield, which I doubt, as they look as if they hardly have a cent to buy beans let alone guns! It's jest as well thet you have me, Webster, to help ya out! I brought extra guns with me. They kin have them after they're stretched out dead in the snow. It needs to look convincing. The goddamned sheriff ain't stupid – might even be smarter than you! But not . . .' Heston smiled, looking straight into Parker's eyes, 'as smart as me. I kin see a couple of aces hidden under any feller's hand.'

Parker made no answer to the jeer and said nothing further as Heston brought his followers into the house, where they lounged in the armchairs, grinning like apes, and drank the whiskey from the sideboard. Immediately afterwards, though, he sent Crow into Oakfield with instructions to find Luke and his friends and to give them the friendly note he had written.

Crow rode into Oakfield by the saddleback hill, which he well knew to be the best route in winter. His face held an expression of worry as he rode through the snow for he was troubled by the sudden appearance of the four evil-looking men who accompanied Heston. He had seen them before, drinking and causing trouble in town, and he knew them to be no good. On the other hand, he was well aware that Mr Webster needed help against the gang of strangers who had been following him with their minds on revenge. It was necessary to deal with them promptly and without seeking the help of the law. Mr Webster had said all that and had been supported by Gus whom Crow looked up to as an elder brother and a wiser man than himself.

Nevertheless, the prospect of aligning himself with Heston's men depressed him greatly and it was with misgivings that he rode into town to search for the party of strangers.

He found them easily enough for they had already aroused comment in the town, where any stranger rapidly became a topic of conversation. He was familiar enough with the Low Dog saloon and informed the barkeeper of his errand. He shortly found himself facing the young feller called Luke, who did not seem as desperate a character as he had been led to believe.

Not that much was said between them. Crow handed over the note with a grimace that was supposed to be the friendly smile Webster had instructed him to put on. Luke accepted it and glanced at Crow as if seeking some explanation. Crow shrugged and turned away quickly to ride out of town without delay, while Luke opened up the missive with a puzzled expression.

Some distance beyond the town limits Crow met Eddie Hunt. They knew one another of old and halted to exchange greetings as they had always done. Eddie was riding into town to collect a few supplies but evinced more interest than usual when he saw Crow, as there had been something on his mind for some days past. Eddie had seen Web with his friends in the town and had been struck by the resemblance he still had in his mind of Harry Webster in the years gone by. It was not a resemblance he had noted in the face of the man who had claimed to be Harry Webster a short time before. Sure, many years had passed and people change but of the two Eddie would have picked out the down-and-out feller who called himself Web rather than the guy in the new sheepskin coat as being the man who had got into trouble all that time past and had left Goldcrest under a cloud.

Eddie could see that his friend Crow was worried. He had it written all over him. With a little prompting, Crow told him of his errand, though not of the actual contents of the letter, which he did not know himself. He also mentioned Heston and the scumbags from the shack over the other side of the valley and how they had congregated at the ranch. At that, Eddie pricked up his ears. He was of a more suspicious nature than Crow and could smell a rat better than any mongrel with an empty belly and a lack of sympathy for vermin.

7

When Jenny Spence reached her cabin she
closed the door behind her as if to shut out the
world. She felt greatly troubled and banked up
the fire with hands that trembled a little so that
she burned her fingers and put them in her
mouth as if she were a child before she gripped
her nerves and looked at the situation in a
calmer way.

She thought of the conversation she had had
with Luke, who seemed to her to be a decent
man once she had seen through his shabby
appearance. The tale of the mining accident had
caught her attention and his description of the
state of mind of Web made her stare quickly at
the sick man as if he were a ghost from the past,
before turning her head away.

She had not looked hard at Web. For some

reason she could not do so, but he had stared at her throughout the discussion, as if she were a person half-remembered from a dream.

Now, in the seclusion of her cabin, she thought of him more carefully and knew that his grey eyes matched those that looked out at her from her mirror every morning and that his mouth, too, was like her own. His voice, as he had called out 'Anne' after her retreating figure, was still with her, heavy in its significance. It was her mother's name and she shared something of her mother's looks as well as those of her father.

She remembered too her mother's words and what had been said to her by Eric Webster only weeks before he died. In those few conversations with Eric, he had spoken to her as he had never spoken before. Gone was the dislike he had always shown for her. It had been replaced by understanding and he had told her things that she had never known and given her something that had made her gasp in surprise.

Slowly the realization dawned that the man in Oakfield whose mind was almost empty of the past was her own father – a man of whom she had had no kind thought since the day when she had learned that Jeremy Spence was a figment of her mother's imagination only.

There had been hatred for this man whom

she now knew to be her father but had never seen. It seemed to her that he had cast her and her mother aside, although she knew that he had gone away before she had been born. Now, however, seeing that pitiable figure in Oakfield, she had felt her hatred and anger dissipating, leaving a confused sense of emptiness.

Like Crow and Gus she had looked out for the return of Harry Webster and had seen the man who had ridden through the snow from Oakfield that day as they had. She, however, had remained at her distance and had never seen him close to.

Now it came to her that she wanted to see him. She had no idea who he was but it seemed that he had come to take over Harry Webster's position. No doubt he meant to have Goldcrest for himself. She made up her mind to see him tomorrow, not to tell him anything or to question him, but just to see for herself what kind of a man he was.

Then she would know what to do. She believed she might remain silent on the one thing she knew but he did not.

The next day dawned bright and clear but she still hesitated and did not ride out until much of the morning had gone by. Before then, Luke and Web and their two friends had already journeyed much of the way to Goldcrest, not by the saddleback hill, because they did not know the short route, but the long way by the river which brought them almost into sight of the ranch a little before the appointed hour of midday.

Luke carried the letter he had received from the rancher in the pocket of his jacket. It was a polite, businesslike and almost friendly letter. Parker had been at pains to make it so. In it he admitted that the sick man did have a relationship of a kind with Goldcrest and that it needed to be seriously discussed so that he could benefit from it. For that reason, it would be worthwhile if the whole party could come to the ranch to meet that fine lawyer, Mr Elliot Bowmaster, who would lay the entire case open to them and settle matters to everyone's satisfaction.

Luke was quite impressed with the letter. He had, of course, never heard of any lawyer called Elliot Bowmaster but he sounded like a man who might know what he was talking about. Parker had never heard of any such lawyer either but he knew the value of such details when writing something intended to deceive At the end, the rancher apologized for not knowing the names of the gentlemen to whom he was writing, except of course for the one person already alluded to. This gentleman would, in particular, be pleasantly surprised when he discovered his true place in the scheme of things. The letter was signed with a good natured and confident flourish: *Harry Webster!*

In spite of the tone of the letter, however, Luke was not without suspicion. He remembered the reaction of the rancher outside the bank when he had set eyes on Web and the way the man had hurried away as if he had something to hide. Still, he might have had a change of heart and decided to lay the facts bare so that Web and his friends would be satisfied. It seemed to Luke that Web must be related to the family of Websters – possibly a cousin. Certainly he bore a resemblance to the girl called Jenny Spence, but neither of them looked much like the Harry Webster who had come out of the bank and had later written this fine letter.

It all seemed a real mix-up but maybe today all would be explained. Luke certainly hoped so but he was glad enough to have his Colt at his side, a weapon he was determined to use if he felt he had to.

At Goldcrest, Heston had made his preparations with some care. The killing ground he had chosen was the open space between the main house and the stables and large barn. The stables were directly opposite, the barn a little to one side. It would be an easy matter to create a field of fire from these three directions, hoping to mow down the hicks from Smoky Hill in a matter of a very few minutes. Then the bodies could be spread out a bit to make it look as if they had been mounting an attack and any of them without a gun could be given one to ensure that in the eyes of the law they appeared as a bunch of desperadoes.

Very soon after that, Heston intended clearing off with his henchmen, stopping only to collect his money from the rancher. He had no wish to see representatives of the law or to be involved in any investigation. That had never been Heston's scene. There was too much in his past life that could not stand the light of day.

He and Parker and Gus and one of the hired killers were stationed in the house where they had a clear view of the open stretch of slush between it and the stables. Crow and another man crouched in the stables, rifles at the ready. The barn was manned by the two remaining assassins. Both of these kept a sharp look-out through the door, but were already impatient as they chewed tobacco and cursed the cold and the delay.

Shortly before midday Parker looked sharply out of the window as he saw the girl coming into sight from behind a snow-covered hillock in the middle distance. He recognized her at once as the girl who lived in the cabin about a mile away, who had looked at him with undisguised hostility and to whom he had never spoken. She was riding her white pony and stared straight ahead as if she had something important on her mind.

'Who the hell's that?' asked Heston in exasperation. 'Get rid of her, fer God's sake!'

Parker stepped out on to the porch as the girl rode slowly across the designated place of death. She brought her pony to a halt and she and Parker stared at one another for a few seconds. Parker jumped visibly as he found himself looking into the eyes of Harry Webster and Jenny's mouth tightened as she fully realized that she was not looking at Harry.

They said nothing. It had been in Jenny's mind to say something about the rental for her cabin. She had never paid rent but she had felt she needed some excuse, however flimsy, for coming over to see the rancher. Now, she suddenly felt that it did not matter. She could not bring herself to speak to this man. She turned her pony aside to ride away.

From the window Heston allowed his eyes to drift from observing Parker's meeting with the girl to the distant horizon, on which he had been keeping a close eye for some time. Suddenly he realized there was movement there, a tiny lump of colour against the snow, moving with what seemed infinite slowness.

'Riders!' he yelled. 'They're coming! Git the girl! Git her!'

'Right!' Cornhusk, the Indian half-breed standing beside him, grinned and raised his rifle. 'I'll git the bitch . . .'

Heston pushed the rifle to the floor.

'Not that way, you goddamned fool! These guys will hear the shot from this distance, no trouble! Petrie!' He shouted over to the stable opposite where a face had appeared at the door-way. 'Git thet gal! Git hold of her! Tie her up or somethin'!'

Petrie, small but wiry with skin like dirty sand-paper under his ragged beard, darted from his hiding-place and grabbed at Jenny before she could spur her pony into flight. His rough hands gripped her clothing and he pulled her to the ground where she struggled for a moment in the wet snow before her hands were held firmly behind her back and she was dragged into the dark interior of the stable. The horses in the stalls at the rear moved restlessly at the distur-bance. Crow stared in horror. He had always had a liking and a respect for the girl although she had made little attempt to show friendship towards him.

'No use fightin'. A man's gotcha now an' ya cain't git away nohow!' Petrie snatched a short length of rope from the floor to tie Jenny's hands and shoved her into a corner. 'Don't try anything unless ya want a pistol-whipping! Too bad if we have to make thet pretty face of yours look like minced calf-brains.' He leered at her from close quarters, his foul breath in her nostrils. 'I reckon you and me kin git along real swell later when we ain't so busy.'

'Hey! Leave her be! There's no call to be knocking Miss Spence around like thet!' Crow was finding his voice after the shock of seeing her manhandled so roughly. 'Git back from her!'

His rifle was pointing at Petrie but the cowpuncher just stared at him without fear, amused contempt showing in his eyes.

'Cut it out, bonehead, we got a job to do. If ya really want to fight me we kin git to it later but ya won't survive. I've buried more guys like you than tongue kin tell.'

Breathing hard, Crow turned away to peer over the lower part of the stable door. Things were beginning to smell bad. It seemed to have been just an unfortunate chance that had brought Jenny Spence into this dangerous situation and he wished with all his heart that it had not happened. These guys that Major Heston had brought with him were the lowest of the low and it was a terrible thing to see the young woman suddenly brought into captivity, however short a time she might be held.

'Miss Spence,' he said, glancing over his shoulder at her as she crouched in the corner, 'I'm real sorry about this. The thing is, though, that we're waiting to settle things with a gang of roughnecks who are planning to kill Mr Webster. It seems the only way it kin be done! If you could jest sit quiet and keep well down outa—'

'Why don't you shut your big mouth?' snapped Petrie. 'You got too much to say.'

'Mr Webster?' asked Jenny. 'Do you mean Harry Webster?'

'Yeah, Harry—'

'Close your mouth, gal, or I'll close it permanent,' snarled Petrie, threatening her with his rifle. 'And you too, dumbhead.' He prodded Crow with the muzzle. 'Keep your goddamned eyes to the front. The bastards are coming!'

No more was said in the stable. Crow bit his lip, angry and confused. Petrie and the other men whom Major Heston had brought with him were like low criminals, worse by far than the young guy he had seen briefly in Oakfield when he had delivered the letter. Still, Harry Webster and the major and even Gus were convinced that the gang approaching over the snow were a bad bunch, out to commit murder for the sake of revenge, and this trap was the only way to deal with them. He believed he could do nothing else but go along with it, even though it was beginning to smell like a skunk in the kitchen. He scowled and muttered under his breath while Jenny remained still, her mind turning over as she attempted to work things out.

Out over the snow-covered trail, Luke kept his eyes on the house as it gradually seemed to loom larger against the backdrop of white. He was impressed by its size and fine architecture. It seemed to dwarf the other buildings nearby, the stables and barns and worksheds. Beyond, the partly frozen river gleamed under the blue of the cold sky.

It took quite a while to cover the distance between themselves and the ranch but Luke's eyes never wavered. At last he saw what he had expected, which was the figure of the rancher appearing on the step of the porch just in front of the building. The man waved in a friendly manner like a host welcoming guests.

Web sat up straight in the saddle. His eyes were suddenly brighter than they had been for weeks. They contained a sense of wonder mixed with bewilderment almost like a sleeper awakening.

Catfish looked all round as they approached. Something of his former way of thinking as an old-time Plains Indian had returned to his mind in recent days and there was caution and an instinct for danger now that he had not felt for many years. He noticed the number of horse-tracks in the snow. Then he saw the girl's pony, fully saddled but wandering.

'Something' ain't jest right,' he grunted. 'Better take things easy, Luke.'

But Web was urging his mount forward. Excitement showed in his face. The sight of Goldcrest was beginning to stir his mind. Vague memories of voices and faces from the past seemed to be struggling to the surface. His hands trembled as he tightened his grip on the reins.

'Goldcrest! Jeeze! Hey, Eric!' His voice rose almost to a shout. 'Hey, I'm back! Harry's back!'

His horse bounded forward under the pressure from his heels. Very quickly he was within a short distance of the ranch buildings. At the sight of him Parker stepped hastily back inside the house. It was almost an instinctive movement. To see the man he had attempted to murder riding towards him, shouting and waving was an unnerving experience. Also, Parker was only too well aware of the fusillade of shots that would be released at any moment and had no wish to be in the firing-line.

Luke saw the movement and his suspicions were confirmed.

'Web! Hold back, Web!' he yelled but Harry Webster's excitement had taken him beyond listening.

Inside the stables and the barn and the main house rifles were raised. Petrie grinned in expectation. Crow tensed, his mind still uncertain. Jenny Spence, finding herself no longer stared at by her captor, straightened herself up to peer through a chink in the timber wall. She saw Harry Webster quite close and the young man called Luke only a little further off.

'Harry!' she shouted, 'Harry! Keep away!

She could have shouted: *Father!* At that exact moment she recognized him fully for what he was. But such a word could not have come to her lips, although she stared at Harry Webster as if seeing him for the first time.

Harry reined in his mount, astonishment and disbelief sweeping into his features.

'Anne!' he shouted. 'Anne!'

The rifle bullet from the house took him in

the shoulder and he fell like a sack of meal to the ground. A short distance behind him, Luke leaped to the snow, realizing that to attempt to ride away would expose his back to the next bullet. Bitty drew hard on the reins, surprised and dismayed. A bullet smashed into his forehead and he fell backwards, spilling blood into the crisp whiteness of a drift piled up against a fence.

Catfish swung his pony savagely to one side and made for a corner of the stables. He reached it just as a red-hot slug ripped across his back.

Inside the stables, Petrie had swung round on Jenny, rifle pointing, his face twisted in fury.

'You goddamned bitch! Now you kin take this in the belly!'

But he did not have time to pull the trigger. Crow's rifle roared in the confined space and Petrie's brains splattered over the timbers of the ceiling while the horses in their stalls nearby whinnied and stamped and pulled at their halters.

8

Luke sprawled in the snow, his body suddenly aching from the fall from his horse, one arm doubled under his chest the other stretched out instinctively to protect his face as he fell. For a moment he lost his breath and he could not move but his mind raced as he tried to work out this new situation.

That they had ridden into an ambush was beyond question. Web lay about twenty yards to his front, having gone down with a rifle bullet from one of buildings just ahead. His body lay in a disfigured heap in the wet, heavily trodden snow. Luke knew that Web had galloped forward as he heard the woman's voice which seemed to have come from the stables over to the left of the open stretch before the house. It had seemed like a warning. The woman had shouted for

Harry to keep back. Harry? Then had come the roar of a rifle from the stables just before the shot that had brought Web to the ground. The woman, Luke felt sure, had suffered the consequences of that warning call.

His heart twisted in despair. Somehow, he knew it was the girl he had met in Oakfield who had attempted to warn Web of the danger – the girl called Jenny. She had been too late in her warning for Web – Harry Webster – had taken that treacherous bullet almost at the same time as she had paid the penalty of her own action.

Bitty was dead too. Luke had seen it happen from the corner of his eye. He had even glimpsed the sudden gush of blood from Bitty's head as he tumbled to the ground. Catfish had vanished. Behind him could be heard only the sounds of horses milling around in the snow in panic.

All this Luke thought in a few seconds. There was no time to ponder about any of this. His own position was one of extreme danger. He lay in the open, an easy target for the next round of gunfire.

He twisted and slithered to one side as a bullet sang close overhead. He dared not rise as to do so would make him an even easier target. There was a stretch of fencing a few yards off. He got to it in a slippery crawl and pushed his entire body into the snow that had piled up behind it. There was no protection except that he was suddenly out of sight from the house. There was nothing at all to stop bullets.

He could not remain here. A slug thumped into a fence post inches from his head. Peering through the snow that almost covered his face, he was able to see the main house clearly and realized he was now a little to one side of it. His only possible chance was to run towards it and seek a position below the line of fire from the windows.

In a second he made up his mind and yanked himself to his feet, leaped over the fence and ran, slipping and stumbling, towards his enemies. There was nowhere else to go. To turn away was suicide. To remain where he was meant death. He reached the timber wall of the side of the house and fell and thumped against it with a sound loud enough to alert the occupants as to his whereabouts.

There was a window overhead about six feet from the ground. Luke had seen nobody there as he ran over the snow but now he heard a muttered curse and knew a man had heard the noise and was ready to deal with it. The barrel of a rifle appeared briefly overhead. Luke held his breath. The slightest sound must give his position away. Silently he drew his Colt from its holster.

He was aware of a terrible anger rising within his heart. His friends had been shot down in a treacherous attack. The girl was almost certainly dead too. They had been drawn into this ambush with a letter of flowery language, deep in its own hypocrisy. Instead of friendship and reasoned discussion the plan had been to kill them all like so many wild animals. He knew it had to do with Web – Harry Webster as he undoubtedly was – and it had all been done to kill Harry and his friends so that the rancher could claim what was not his by right.

The rancher? Suddenly, the vision of Harry as he had been left in that mineshaft came into Luke's mind. It all fitted into place. It had been an act of intended murder. The man at the bank in Oakfield and the man who had appeared at the porch of the house a few minutes ago and the one who had brought down the roof of the mine to kill and silence his partner were one and the same.

There was no longer room for doubt in Luke's mind.

His anger burned like a fire in a barn. It grew in intensity with every second. His grip on his revolver tightened. There were only seconds to spare before the man at the window realized where his enemy was and shot down upon him.

Luke caught a glimpse of clothing at the window-ledge. He leaped up, grabbed at it and found his fingers gripping the lower edge of a jacket. He held tight and threw himself to the ground just as he felt the man lean forward.

His weight brought the man down in a wild rush on top of him. Luke's gun roared, thrusting into the man's chest and releasing its bullet at point blank range. Blood poured over Luke, wetting his face and neck in its sudden warmth. He twisted to one side until the body fell away from him. Then he sprang for the edge of the window to pull himself up and into the room.

In the snow beneath the window Gus groaned in agony and died within seconds.

Luke found himself in a finely furnished room with a desk and padded chairs. The inner door was ajar and he caught sight of figures beyond it. A rifle boomed and red-hot fire drew blood from his shoulder. He fired in return and the vague shapes in the other room vanished.

Then bullets flew like swift hornets through the open doorway. He dropped to the floor and sought cover behind the desk. He had no idea how many men he was up against but he was certain that he could not remain where he was. Even if they were firing almost at random he must be hit within a few seconds . . .

At that same moment Catfish crouched behind the stable, breathing hard as he struggled to get the pain from the wound across his back under control. He could hear the sounds of scared horses moving inside and slightly further off, but scarcely muffled by the buildings themselves, the thunder of gunfire.

He had no gun. Only Luke had been armed and there was little doubt now that the young feller was in the thick of it. Catfish searched desperately for a weapon of some kind as he moved along the back wall of the stables. He came to the corner and, peering round, saw that he was only yards from the barn, which faced across the open space where the shooting had started. The door of the barn was slightly open and Catfish saw two rifles take turns at firing across the same area.

Inside the barn the two half-breeds recruited by Heston crouched with hot rifles in their hands. They had fired at the group of horsemen that had appeared before them and had seen Bitty and Web downed and the Indian of whom their boss had spoken of with such contempt fall wounded from the saddle and struggle in the snow.

Now suddenly there seemed nobody to shoot at so they fired at the loose horses with some idea of making certain that none of the invading party could escape. They hit Bitty's horse and saw it crumple to the ground as the pitiless bullet tore out its heart. The other horses vanished as they galloped off in fear and were shielded by the house and stables.

Catfish ran like a clumsy moose across the intervening space between the stables and the end of the barn. Because of the angle of the barn wall he could not be seen by the two snipers and in a moment he had stumbled into the pile of firewood lying there. To his joy there was a long-handled axe still stuck in a log half-hidden in the snow. He withdrew it silently.

As he did so an age-old sensation came into his mind, sending a surge of passion throughout his spine. He had felt nothing like it for decades but knew that it belonged to an earlier era in his life when he had held such an axe and had used it to deadly effect against warriors whom he had regarded as his enemies.

All sensation of fear left him and the pain of his back went unnoticed. The feel of the axe in his hands suddenly seemed to give him superhuman strength, well beyond what he might have felt even with a superior weapon.

He crept along the barn wall to the doorway. A rifle still peeped out, searching for a target. Catfish did not hesitate. He leaped forward and thrust the door open with his shoulder. A small man with black straggling hair and the dark eyes of an Indian stared up in surprise and horror.

Catfish yelled out a half-remembered war whoop and swung the heavy axe. The blade struck hard into the man's neck. For a second there was no blood and there was no cry at all, just the staring eyes and the open mouth from which no sound came. Then the blood gushed and the man fell silently to the grain-strewn floor, his head suddenly lolling as his half-severed neck sprang open.

From the corner of his eye, Catfish saw the other man, dark-moustached and scowling. A rifle boomed and Catfish felt a thunderbolt enter his body. A red-hot blade of great weight seemed to hang in his heart. But he did not fall immediately. The axe-blade had come free as its victim had sprawled to the ground and now Catfish swung the axe again and struck hard upon the other man's shoulder.

With a pained yell the half-breed stumbled out through the barn door and fell to the snow while the dying Catfish towered over him, axe raised again for the killing stroke. . . .

In the main house, all was confusion. The close gunfight between the occupants of the two rooms thundered on. Luke could see little for gunsmoke and thanked his lucky stars for it because it meant that his opponents would be blinded also.

He did not know for certain how many shots he had fired but knew he must soon reload. That would be the moment when they would fall upon him with their deadly rifle fire. He knew by the sound that at least two of the men facing him were armed with Winchesters and had no need to reload for many more rounds. They might even have been counting how often he had fired and were preparing to press home their attack as soon as they saw his disadvantage.

That time would soon arrive. Luke realized that he had to move. His only chance was to shift his position to a point just beside the door from which he might be able to see into the other room and pick off one of his enemies. It was a desperate move. Even if he killed one there were others, how many he was not sure, ready to fill his body with bullets.

Nevertheless, he crawled from under the heavy desk and ran for the wall by the door. A bullet sang past his face. Then he saw a blurred figure against the light from a window and pressed the trigger of the Colt. The man jumped and cursed but did not fall. Two rifle bullets hammered into the doorpost, forcing Luke to draw back.

For a brief moment there was relative silence, then Luke heard a man's voice roused into fury. Even in the turmoil of his embattled mind, Luke was surprised. He recognized the voice as that of Heston, whom he had last seen in the cabin across the valley. He had not thought to hear that voice again so soon.

'Git thet polecat, fer Chris'sake! There's only one guy in there, ya couple of dumbbells! Hey, Husk! Git in there and finish him! Good Gawd, what's goin' on out there too? There's thet pesky Injun with a goddamned axe! I'll git him!' The sound of his rifle rang out and he grunted in satisfaction. 'Got the bastard!'

It was true. Heston's bullet, fired from an open window, took Catfish in the head and brought him a swifter end than the bloody wound in his chest would otherwise have done.

At that moment, Cornhusk, bleeding from the slight flesh wound made by Luke's last bullet, mind blazing with the fury of pain, carried out the order of his boss and charged into the room beside Luke, determined to finish the business once and for all.

Luke, suddenly caught at close quarters, grappled with the man. For a moment they were too close together to use their firearms but then Cornhusk struck out with his rifle and hit Luke's injured shoulder. Then Luke tripped and fell to the floor.

Cornhusk towered over him, turning his rifle in his hands to get in the final bullet.

'Jeeze!' Heston's voice suddenly contained surprise, consternation and fear. 'Good grief! Thet's it! Hey, Husk, you got thet guy yet!'

'I got him!' yelled Cornhusk triumphantly.

His answer was not meant to be taken literally. He did not mean that he had yet killed Luke. He meant only that Luke was at his mercy.

It was a fatal mistake. Things had changed for Heston. His only thought now was to get out of the unholy mess that had developed, and that meant riding like hell away from Goldcrest and leaving no witnesses to say he had ever been there.

So he shot Curnhusk in the back. His bullet went all the way through and embedded itself in the wall of the room.

Then Heston raced for the outer door and out

on to the veranda. For a moment his eyes flick-
ered again to the eastern horizon to search once
more for the far-off riders he had observed a
moment ago. He knew who they must be – a
bunch of lawmen from Oakfield. Something
about the way they rode told him that. They
came as a compact group with something of
determination in their movement. They had
obviously come around the saddleback hill too,
straight out of town.

Parker had rushed out on to the veranda also,
and now stared with fearful fascination in the
same direction. He too recognized that the
whole plan had fallen to pieces. He turned to
face Heston, his mouth opening as if about to
speak, but Heston spoke first.

'Stupid pig!' he snarled and pulled the trigger
of his rifle. Parker reeled and fell heavily on to
the boards of the veranda, one arm waving wildly
in the air.

Then Heston ran over towards the stables. On
the way he passed the still form of Catfish sprawling partly over the half-breed, who lay in the in
the churned-up and bloody snow. The man
raised his head, opening his mouth in appeal
but Heston shot him at close range and his face
slumped to the ground.

In a further bound, Heston reached the

stables and booted open the door. Before him stood Crow, rifle in hands but undecided as to what to do next. He was given no chance to make up his mind. Heston's bullet sent him staggering across the boards and he fell heavily across the corpse that lay there.

For the briefest of moments, Heston stared at the mess of Petrie's shattered head, then stepped briskly to the stall that held his horse. He did not notice the girl hiding behind the sacks of meal stacked up at the main door of the building. He had, in fact, forgotten all about Jenny Spence in the turmoil of the fight.

In a moment he had led out his already saddled mount and was immediately ready to take flight. He looked around at the killing ground and saw Web and Bitty and Parker, all lying still, and the corpses of Catfish and the man beside him. He decided then that no one was left to tell the tale.

If he could move out unseen by keeping the main house between himself and the posse and could reach the river, he believed he could make his way to a place where he could lie low until he reckoned it was safe to ride by a circuitous route back to his own cabin.

After that he would put on a face of innocence and deny all knowledge of the affair at Goldcrest

– an affair he now wished with all his heart he had never become involved in.

He turned his horse, made his way round the back of the house and set spurs to his mount to make all speed. Thankfully, the weather was changing. Soon there would be snow to cover his tracks.

From the stable door Jenny Spence peered out to see him go. Her whole body was tense. Her hand shook as it held the iron latch. Behind her, two men, one of whom she had known as a friend, lay sprawling in blood on the rough boards. Outside, corpses lay scattered in the snow.

She was sure that no one was left alive. Only Heston could be seen riding away. She looked after him with anger in her eyes and, almost as if he in some strange way felt the hostility of her glance upon the back of his neck, he turned in the saddle to look.

He drew rein. His mount came round and began to trot back to the ranch He drew his revolver.

With a gasp, Jenny slipped back into the place of death. For a moment she hesitated and then went to the nearest stall to bring out a horse, believing she might yet escape.

Her mind was filled with fear as she guessed

Heston's murderous intention. For the moment she forgot the bloodstained rifles lying under the corpses at her feet.

9

Luke felt stunned as he lay under the heavy body of the dead man. He could not guess what had happened to end the terrible hand-to-hand conflict so suddenly. He had heard a shot but had hardly been able to distinguish it from all the others already ringing in his ears. Smoke filled his nostrils. Fresh blood mingled with that of his blood-soaked jacket.

He lay still for a few seconds, unable to move, and then heaved the body of Cornhusk to one side. He looked up, fearful that he would find armed men standing over him, ready to fire.

But there was no one there. The room was empty except for the disturbed furniture, plaster from the walls and a picture lying broken on the floor. He struggled to his feet, gun in hand, and approached the doorway once again.

With the greatest of caution he peered into the other room but saw no sign of movement. The front door was open and icy air drifted in. A table lay overturned and a broken chair was in one corner. Slowly he came to the definite conclusion that there was no one there. No trap was waiting for him.

He could not understand what had happened. Those men had had him almost at their mercy. He could not have survived much longer under their murderous fire but now they had vanished, seemingly out through the main door of the house.

He advanced again with the same caution and looked through one of the windows at the end of the room. He saw the stretch of snow between the buildings as before but now it was churned up into a wet slush. A body lay to one side and Luke's shoulders drooped with dismay as he recognized Web, face down with one arm outstretched. Beyond that, in the cleaner snow, was a huddled lump, which was all that remained of Bitty. To the other side two corpses lay, one sprawling over the other. One was Catfish. Even from that distance his head wound and the bloody mass that was his chest could be clearly seen.

Luke bit his lip. To see Catfish dead was a

bitter blow. Anger rose within him anew. He stepped outside on to the veranda and started as he saw the rancher lying on the boards with a bullet wound through his waistcoat. One hand half-covered the man's face, the other held the butt of a handgun, partly withdrawn from its holster.

Then there came a sound from the building opposite, which he recognized as the stables. It was like the trampling of a scared horse. Then suddenly the door flew open and he saw the girl, pulling at the reins of an animal within. She tugged desperately but was dragged back. The horse was obviously terrified and Luke guessed the reason. It was smelling blood. One or more corpses lay over there too, out of sight from where he stood, but part of the carnage all around.

It seemed that every man mixed up in this gunfight had been killed or had made his escape.

Luke was about to descend the few steps, eager to go to the girl to help, but then held back as he heard the sound of a horse from the other side of the house. Suddenly a horseman came into sight a few yards to his right. Luke recognized the man at once as Heston, eyes set on the stables, gun already in hand.

It was obvious that Heston had seen the girl also and knew she was inside. He trotted over the intervening space and slid from the saddle, evidently intent upon following her into the stable to finish her too.

Without fully intending to do so, Luke yelled out. His uppermost thought was to distract Heston from his immediate plan. Heston swung round and stared at Luke with amazement. For a moment he hesitated as if he were seeing a ghost and then cursed out loud and fired a shot, which went wide due to his shocked state of mind and buried itself in the wooden wall of the house.

It was close enough, though, to make Luke leap for cover behind the thick, oaken board carrying the name of the ranch, which was attached to the railing beside the steps. From there he fired off a shot in return but missed as Heston ducked behind his horse.

For a moment or two Heston was undecided as to his course of action. As he looked over to the east he could see that the sheriff and his posse were approaching rapidly. He could recognize Sheriff Drummond and one or two others who were regular deputies. A little to one side could be seen the small figure of a pesky little runt by the name of Eddie Hunt, who spent a lot of time hanging about in saloons but knew more about the goings on around Oakfield than most other folks.

It was obvious to Heston, as it had been from his first sight of them, that the lawmen were not riding out to Goldcrest for no reason. They were on the look-out for trouble and expected to find it. Somebody had been saying too much and Heston guessed that it had been that blabbermouth, Crow, who had as much to say as a mocking-bird and with about the same degree of sense.

It was good to think that Crow lay in the stable with his chest hammered in by a Winchester rifle bullet fired at close range. It was a crumb of comfort in an otherwise hopeless situation.

The word *hopeless* came into Heston's mind unbidden. For the first time, he realized how bad his situation really was. This interfering coyote from Smoky Hill was still alive and shooting, even though Cornhusk had claimed to have finished him and had even been rewarded with a Heston bullet in the back for his trouble. In addition, the girl was still alive in the stable behind him. That meant two witnesses, one of whom was well known and respected in the valley, who could speak against him and point to the carnage for which he was responsible. There

141

was little time to kill them both before the sheriff and his men rode into Goldcrest. Also, the snow that had been falling a few minutes before had eased off, meaning that even if he rode away his tracks could be easily followed.

For the first time he saw himself as a dead man.

In spite of his arrogance and bluster Heston was not a coward. He had always known that the time would come when he would die under a hail of bullets and had long since made up his mind to go down fighting. For the moment he did not move but remained standing behind his horse, which he held tightly by the reins and which now served as a shield from Luke's next bullet.

'Luke Coyle, you some kind of yeller-belly?'

Luke jumped at the unexpected question. For a second he did not know how to answer. It was a thought that had caused him some heart-searching in the past but had not been in his mind for some time. Then he felt the blood on his clothing and the pain of his bullet-grazed flesh and he knew the answer.

'I don't believe so,' he yelled back.

'Yeah? How come you're hiding behind thet board instead of coming out to fight like a man? Let's have you out here in front of me and we'll fight it out, eye-to-eye, gun-to-gun!'

Luke narrowed his eyes, well aware of the trap. Heston had the reputation of being pretty quick on the draw. Such a duel could only give him the advantage.

'You cain't hold thet horse there much longer,' he shouted in answer. 'It ain't like this here board. Why should you be given a better chance when you've gunned down my friends like you did? Did you ask them for a fair fight?'

'I'll tell you why you oughta take me up on this, Coyle. It's because of thet girl in this here stable. I kin be in there in ten seconds, before you kin draw a bead. I'll kill her – take my word on it! And I ain't got any time to talk about this. Thet bunch of lawmen will be here in no time. Git thet into your head! Come out right now or the girl gits it afore you do!'

Luke glanced quickly through the railing to his left and saw the group of horsemen in the distance. He was surprised, as he had not been aware of their approach at all. Now he realized fully the reason for Heston's challenge and he knew also that the man meant what he said. Heston had nothing to lose. He would certainly kill either Jenny or Luke – both if he had time.

There seemed to be no argument. Heston could be in through the swing-doors of the stables almost before Luke could pull the trigger. A lucky shot might bring him down but it was just as likely to miss and then Jenny would die.

Luke saw that he must accept the challenge. To remain where he was while Jenny was murdered could only prove that the jeer of *yellerbelly* was an accurate one.

'All right!' he shouted. 'Leave the girl alone and I'll face you.'

Heston backed off a little to one side to a point where he could not be easily shot in the back from the stable. He was not unaware that the girl might gather her courage and attempt to use one of the guns lying on the bloody floor inside. Now he was shielded from any attack from that direction by the heavy door itself, which could not be pushed open without him having a few seconds' warning. He waited then until Luke rose from his hiding-place and came down the steps of the house.

The horse moved out of the way as soon as Heston released it. Now they stood face to face. Guns had been replaced into their holsters but hands hovered ready to draw.

From the corner of his eye Heston glanced very quickly into the middle distance where the party from Oakfield was showing up much more clearly. The uppermost thought in his mind was to kill Luke and, he hoped, the girl, before downing as many of the sheriff's men as he could.

After that, Major Heston would be no more. He would die as an officer and a gentleman. The fact that he had never attained any such rank and had been a lowly corporal in his army days did not occur to him. It was a lie that had been with him for a long time and he had come to believe it.

Luke was standing a few yards away, face tense, hands twitching slightly. Heston grinned. This could be the last amusing moment of his life. He could see that his opponent was not an experienced gunfighter. The young feller might have guts but it took more than that to survive a gun duel.

At that moment Jenny peered over the top of the stable door. She had given up any idea of making an escape on horseback. The horse she had been struggling with had backed into its stall and the others were snorting and pulling at their halters in their anxiety. Much more important, she knew that Heston was just outside. She had heard his voice although she had not caught the sense of his words.

She could see across the open space to the

veranda of the house opposite where the large notice still proudly proclaimed the name of the ranch. A few yards in front of the steps but a little to the left stood Luke. She knew at once by his demeanour that he was facing Heston, who must be at the corner of the stables just out of her line of sight.

She realized instantly that they were about to engage in a fight to the death. Her first impulse was to call out to Luke not to fight a duel with a man with such a reputation for gunplay, but she closed her mouth tightly, knowing that the slightest distraction would spell death for him.

'Now's your big chance to save your lady friend!' Heston's voice, loud and jeering, made her tremble in a mixture of fear and anger. 'Let's see what a goddamned medical orderly kin do! Brought your stretcher?'

Jenny turned away from the door. She searched for a rifle beneath one of the corpses on the floor and shuddered as she put her hands on the stock, wet and sticky with blood.

Outside, Heston stared fixedly at Luke. There was a question coming into his mind. How many bullets had Luke used up in the house and had he remembered to reload? Maybe he had or maybe not.

'Hey, Luke, you got any bullets left in thet old Colt? Did ya remember to check it?'

Luke's head suddenly jerked in surprise and Heston knew at once that the reloading had not been attended to. There had been little time since the constant firing in the house but an experienced gunman would have found a few seconds to make certain that the chamber of the gun was full.

'Draw!' yelled Heston suddenly. He knew he was about to take a gamble, or there might be one bullet remaining, but he wanted to see real fear in Luke's eyes and he felt the risk was worth it.

Luke drew quickly and pulled the trigger. There was no sound but the click of an empty gun. Heston had already drawn and held Luke in his sight as an easy target but he did not fire. He smiled, his gun held steady.

'Now thet's real careless, Lukey boy! I guess they don't call you "Lucky Boy" because I don't believe you've ever had any – certainly not now. You've got five seconds to live. It's all I kin offer you, as time is pressing and all . . .'

He stared into Luke's eyes, searching for the fear of death, ready to delight in it, ready to gloat for a few seconds of the short life that remained to himself, but he saw no hint of it, only a look of stone that suppressed any suggestion of fear.

Heston's own eyes changed their expression. Now they turned hard and empty, snakelike and without pity – the look of the gunfighter about to deal out death.

Luke did not move. To do so would not save him and it would seem like a move prompted by fear. He felt afraid but was determined to show none of it. His thoughts were less on himself than on the girl. He hoped and prayed that somehow the party from Oakfield would arrive in time to prevent her death.

On the boards of the veranda Parker stirred. For some moments he had been drifting to the surface from the sea of unconsciousness in which he had been submerged. As he looked between the railings surrounding the veranda he could dimly make out the figures of two men standing only a few yards away.

He knew they were both enemies. The man nearest to him had his back turned and was remembered only vaguely; the other he recognized as Heston, whose bullet he now carried. The pain of his wound aroused hatred in his heart more intense than he had ever known in his life. He pushed himself up a little from the boards and thrust his revolver between two of

148

the wooden rails. He steadied his hand against the timber and pulled the trigger.

The bullet sang past Luke and embedded itself in Heston's chest. It seemed to explode within, destroying the heart and lungs and forcing a fountain of blood into the throat and mouth. Heston fell with no sound except for a scarcely audible moan. His limbs were slack and sprawled on impact with the ground like those of a fresh carcass that somehow falls from a butcher's hook. In a second his figure was reduced to a crumpled mass that seemed never to have been a living man.

Jenny stared from the stable door. She held a rifle in her hands but knew it would not be needed for Heston. She could not see his body from where she was but could see the reaction of Luke to the sudden shot.

He had swung round to face the veranda but darted to one side as if in anticipation of another attack. Jenny stared over at Parker but saw him slump back to the boards while his gun slipped from his fingers.

In a moment she was out through the doors of the stables and was running over the snow. As she went she turned the gun in her hands to point at Heston's prone form, but was confirmed in her knowledge that there was no need.

Then she stopped. Luke had turned and was staring in her direction. His heart still trembled. As he had stood under the threat of the gun he had known fear such as he had never experienced in his life before but he had given no outward sign of it. His eyes had met those of the killer but had not flinched beneath that pitiless gaze.

Now he looked at Jenny and knew that she rejoiced to see that he still lived. His own inner being began to sing too in his relief at seeing her unharmed. They looked at one another in silence but did not smile.

To smile was not possible in the midst of the human tragedy surrounding them.

10

The men from Oakfield arrived and looked around at the place of slaughter in disbelief. Questions were asked and answers given but further explanations left to another time. There seemed little inclination to talk. The presence of so much death had a sobering effect upon all who were present. Luke went to Bitty and straightened out his body in the snow. The face under the matted, blood-filled hair looked peaceful, as if he had not had the faintest inkling of what might have happened.

Catfish lay scowling in an angry death. Luke drew him away from the body of his last enemy and put him on his back so that he looked at the sky. He tried to close the eyes but the lids seemed already too cold and the old Indian remained staring in anger at the dark snow-clouds as if somehow all his enemies of the past had taken refuge behind them.

Luke paused then, feeling a dreadful sense of despair. He asked himself why these terrible events had taken place. He turned round to look towards the place where Web still lay crumpled in the snow. It had all been to do with Web. Catfish and Bitty and he, himself, had taken up Web's cause without fully understanding it. Web had not understood it either. That much was evident.

He saw that Jenny had turned and had walked to the spot where Web lay. She was looking down at the still form. There was a curious stillness about her, so much so that he wondered whether she was hovering on the edge of a state of shock now that the danger had passed.

With that thought in mind he strode quickly to her and stood by her side. For a moment she seemed unaware of his presence, then she turned to him, her eyes uncertain, as if she were searching into her own soul for the answer to the same question that had been weighing down his own heart. When she spoke it was in a voice scarcely audible, as if she did not want the other men to hear.

'Look what he scratched in the snow as he died! See, he wrote "Anne" there. You can see it just by his right hand. That was my mother's name.'

'I know, at least, I guessed that before,' answered Luke in a subdued tone.

'I think he still loved her,' went on Jenny softly. 'He never forgot her. I always used to think that he had. He was my father. I never told anyone before. I didn't even know it myself until my mother told me about him. Then I thought he had just ridden away and left her. Eric told me the same kind of thing.'

She looked at him sharply as if wondering whether she had been understood. At that moment, Sheriff Drummond appeared beside them, rugged, moustached face grave, like a man bearing bad news.

'Excuse me, Miss Spence, you all right? Well, thet feller up there on the veranda, he's dying, sure as guns. Thing is, now he says his name's Parker – Jed Parker. He has a watch with his name engraved on it too. He says he was jest trying to take the place of Harry Webster so as to git the ranch and everything. He admits that he tried to kill Harry and thet Harry's lying dead, right here! Kin thet be right?'

Jenny looked startled then she nodded slowly.

'I believe it is,' she said. 'This is the real Harry Webster lying at our feet.'

153

'He says he tried to kill Harry in a gold-mine by explosives. Brought down the roof on his head . . . but Harry survived, like as if it was some miracle.'

'He did,' put in Luke, 'Harry lived through thet but lost his memory. He was only just starting to get it back when this pack of wolves killed him finally.'

Jenny's face had whitened. She looked at the sheriff, then at Luke, before turning quickly away and starting to walk towards the house. She walked slowly at first as if trying to make up her mind and then suddenly quickened her pace. As she climbed the few steps to the porch, Luke saw her draw something from the pocket of her jacket. He followed quietly and stood near to her.

The two men bending over Parker moved back to make room for her. They had been thinking about attempting to carry Parker into the house but knew that his wound was fatal and the movement might kill him at once. Jenny bent over the dying man. She saw but did not touch the silver watch hanging twisted on its chain from his waistcoat. The name 'J. Parker' could be clearly discerned.

'Can you see well enough to read?' She put the question to the dying man with no hint of pity. Her tone was brittle. Anger still burned beneath her words. 'No? All right, then listen. This letter was written more than a year ago to Eric Webster. It's from a lawyer representing the Goldcrest Mining Company and it states that the mining venture has folded up and all the money invested in it has been lost. That includes this ranch. Eric had mortgaged the whole place in the hope of salvaging the gold-mines. Everything has really belonged to the bank since before Eric died. There was never a cent in it for you in spite of all your scheming and killing! I just thought you might like to know that everything you did was just spitting in the wind. You wasted your own life as well as others just for nothing at all!'

She stood up straight and looked down into Parker's eyes as he struggled to open them. A flicker of understanding gleamed for a second beneath the drooping lids. A faint moan came from his lips.

For a moment the faintest suggestion of a smile crept into the corners of her mouth. She was glad he knew but there was no way she could gloat over a dying man. Instead, tears came into her own eyes as she turned away.

Luke held her arm as she came down the steps. They walked a short distance while she struggled to regain her composure and he tried to make sense of what he had heard.

'It's all quite true,' she said at last. 'The thing is, Eric never did forgive Harry for taking Anne from him and for injuring him in the gunfight all those years ago. When he realized he was dying from his illness, he contacted Harry through a newspaper and then wrote and pretended that all was forgiven. He wanted his brother to come back here expecting to inherit everything only to find there was nothing. A sweet revenge! It suited too when the bank decided not to foreclose immediately when they found out about Eric's condition. Eric told me all that and I went along with it because I hated Harry so much at that time.But I don't now,' she continued quietly. 'I saw that day in Oakfield that he wasn't the monster I had imagined. He was obviously ill and I had already guessed that the man at Goldcrest was an impostor.'

'So all this was for nothing,' said Luke. 'It was all just for revenge at the start and then for the greed of money. But there was never anything here at all! If only . . .'

He was about to say more but changed his mind. She looked at him closely, her eyes smiling for the first time.

'Not even for me as the last in line in the family, you're thinking! I never cared about that and I care even less now.' She glanced over to where her pony had wandered into sight beyond the stables, and her voice changed into a tone of weariness. 'I guess I've been here long enough. The place sickens me. I want to get away.'

He caught her pony for her and helped her to mount. For a second their hands touched and he gazed up at her. Her features were calm now. A tiny smile hovered at the edges of her mouth.

'What are you goin' to do now?' he asked.

'I'll get back to Oakfield as soon as I can. I have work there in the hotel and I can get a room easily. I won't be back to Goldcrest, ever. What about you?'

'Well, I'll have to stick around for a little while. There are friends to bury and all kinds of things to discuss with the sheriff. Then I'll ride back to Smoky Hill. There's a woman I need to look after.'

'Oh,' she looked surprised and her lips tightened a little.

'Her name's Mary Elk. Thet's her husband over there, looking at the sky. I can't do anything for Bitty's folks because he lost them a long time ago but Catfish's widow will need a bit of help. We need to salvage what we kin out of every mess thet is made by crazy men who think thet killing is the only way.'

'Like the war,' she suggested quietly, looking

into his eyes. It was as if she knew more about the workings of his mind than he would have imagined.

'Thet's it . . . jest like the war. But after I've been to Smoky, I'll be back. Oakfield seems all right to me. Maybe I kin make something of myself there.'

'I'll keep a look out for you.' She smiled. 'Tell you what, though, get your hair cut, just for a start . . . you could look pretty smart if you really thought about it!'

He grinned and held on to her hand much more firmly this time.

'It'll be a transformation!' he said. 'Keep your eyes peeled next summer for the *dude* from Smoky!'

She laughed and rode away, pausing only to wave to him through the lightly falling snowflakes.